I0545546

Spellbinding Blend

A PARAMOUR BAY MYSTERY
BOOK SIX

KENNEDY LAYNE

KENNEDY LAYNE PUBLISHING, INC.

Dedication

Jeffrey & Cole — I love you!

About the Book

This is one spellbinding tale of magical chaos you won't want to miss in the continuation of USA Today Best-selling Author Kennedy Layne's cozy paranormal mystery series...

The flowers are in bloom, the songbirds are singing, and the tourists have begun to flock to the small coastal town of Paramour Bay for the Spring Festival. All is going according to plan, but Raven Marigold has one itsy-bitsy loose end to tie up regarding a possible warlock posing as one of the townsfolk. There has to be a simple solution, right?

Well, one itsy-bitsy loose end turns into two...maybe three...when a body is found behind the kissing booth at the traveling carnival on the edge of town. When Raven discovers a connection between the victim and the warlock she's been keeping a close eye on, she and her trusty familiar will have no choice but to take the case. After all, it wouldn't do to have the residents know that magic exists!

Grab a ticket and take a ride on this swirling mystery that will leave you dizzy with misleading clues, magical chaos, and a spellbinding blend that doesn't quite go according to plan!

One

The small coastal town of Paramour Bay, Connecticut, had been awakened with a single yellow bloom around two weeks ago in the courthouse flowerbed. I'd witnessed the dawn of a new season myself after filling out some paperwork for the tea shop with the city. The days that followed had been straight out of the pages of a fairytale.

Bright, vivid colors had burst forth in rows upon rows in the various planters, songbirds had returned to fly gracefully overhead from branch to budding branch, and the hint of warmth that carried on the gentle breezes had shown a welcome respite from the cool weather.

Spring had finally arrived after a harsh, bitter winter, and it was as if new beginnings were being offered to anyone with a wish to have one. Nothing could forestall the waves of vibrant energy surging through the air.

Except those conniving squirrels. Look at them sitting in that tree, rubbing their hands together, scheming. They do this every year. It's an ongoing battle between us. They're up to something catastrophic. I just know it.

Leave it to Leo, my familiar, to ruin my spring-has-arrived moment.

I didn't bother to reply as I continued to smile at the numerous early-bird tourists and joyful residents passing by my booth's presentation while enjoying the sunshine, the sights, and the company. Some even poured themselves a few samples from the carafes of the tea and coffee I'd steeped and brewed to perfection. I was pretty sure I had gained some new customers after today's social gathering.

Leo and I were currently minding our vendor's booth for my tea shop—*Tea, Leaves & Eves*—at Paramour Bay's annual Spring Festival. Technically, I ran a tea and coffee shop after incorporating some premium coffee blends, and I was seriously considering changing its name to *Tea, Leaves & Grounds*.

The festival was quite the attraction for this Norman Rockwell replica of a small New England seaside village, population of three hundred and thirty-five. It was our way of kicking off the official start of the annual tourist season, with a dash of fun thrown in for those passing through to see the bay.

I think they forgot the fun part. Let's get back to these squirrels...

All those cute little squirrels were doing was trying to find some peace within all the commotion and excitement that had occurred in the past few days. I couldn't say I blamed them. It was a bit hectic. They'd taken to running, jumping, and hiding in the trees scattered around the park. They probably wouldn't come down until everything returned to normal after the lights went out after this busy weekend.

The festival's committee had even hung a large white sign at the entrance of town announcing the celebration and hired a traveling carnival, which had been set up in the open field across from the park. My table was literally at the end of

Oceanview Drive, giving me the perfect view of the ticket booth and entry gate into the carnival.

I couldn't have asked for a better location to advertise my tea shop, and I'm pretty sure I had Sheriff Liam Drake to thank for such a coveted spot in the drawing. As I'd mentioned before, I currently have a few samples left of my bestselling hot teas and some select coffee blends set out in Yeti urns next to a stack of to-go cups with my logo emblazoned on the sides. We also displayed an assortment of beverage-related devices that would catch any potential buyer's attention. There was little left in the way of stock items behind me, but it was almost time to pack up anyway. I was looking forward to enjoying the festival's live folk music entertainment being provided by the carnival.

I'd say the turnout had been quite a success, all told.

A quick perusal of the gathering crowd showed that Liam wasn't anywhere in sight. I tried to bury my disappointment, especially since we hadn't been able to spend much time together this past week. Seeing as he was Paramour Bay's only police presence, aside from the small three-man unarmed security detail the carnival operator provided, Liam would be working around the clock for the next couple of days to ensure that the residents and tourists had a safe weekend. One would think with all the spells and enchantments in the family grimoire that I could squeeze out a few moments of time.

I wish those annoying squirrels would stand still. All their twitching is very annoying. They're giving me a headache with all their incessant chattering.

"Why does Leo look like he's ready to attack someone?"

Heidi Connolly suddenly claimed the second foldout chair that had been designated for my table by the town's festival committee, her blonde curls bouncing with the abrupt downward motion. In her hand was a paper funnel full of warm

3

candied almonds that she'd been talking about buying all day long. I leaned back in my seat and held out my hand, needing a sugar pick-me-up myself.

"He's upset that the squirrels are fidgeting in the trees behind us." I popped a candied almond that my best friend had somewhat reluctantly relinquished into my mouth, taking a moment to relish the delicious sweet snack that practically melted in my mouth. I instantly reached for another one before she could withdraw the treat and save them all for herself. "We're both in bad moods, and that won't change unless we can unilaterally prove that Rye Dolgiram isn't a warlock. Did you find out anything while you were standing in line? I saw him talking to one of the carnival workers for a bit, but the man walked away afterward with a brochure in his hand."

The reason I was able to ask such a question was that the food truck serving an assortment of candied nuts and fruits was parked directly behind Rye's table. He was known well enough around town that he didn't need to solicit customers for his handyman business, but he'd gone ahead and reserved one of the vendor tables anyway, as had nearly every other business in town. I guess the same could be said for me, but he technically didn't have a brick-and-mortar shop to advertise. He'd been passing out brochures to the local residents, and even some to those in neighboring towns.

"I didn't find out anything," Heidi reluctantly admitted, tilting her head to the side while she studied the man in question. There was no denying the fact that he was tall, dark, and handsome. He was also the type that a woman inherently knew was harboring a deep, dark secret. With that said, he went out of his way to be kind and inordinately helpful to those residents around town. "Raven, I'm thinking that what Leo saw the night Rye fixed your gate was nothing more than a trick of the light. I don't think he used magic, and I don't believe he's actually a warlock."

Heidi could have a point. I did say that I might have hallucinated the entire thing, given my level of catnip consumption that day. Hey, what do you think would happen to those squirrels if I stuffed catnip in their acorns?

"Leo, stop spying on the wildlife and focus on our target."

Who says the squirrels aren't our targets? They might not be on your radar, but they're certainly on mine. Come to think of it, they might just be in league with Rye.

To say that the last eight weeks or so have been lived with a fair amount of stress would be an understatement. It had been that long since Leo thought he'd witnessed Rye use arcane magic outside my cottage to defeat one of Nan's minor protective wards.

It was a wonder I hadn't developed an ulcer.

The mere possibility that the man could be a warlock had me all worked up. Trust me when I say that there would be a fair ration of ramifications if that were the case. You see, I was a descendant of a long line of witches who had been expelled from our previous coven for consorting with humans.

My family had been excommunicated from a notorious coven located in Windsor, but word had it that the council was on the brink of war. I wanted no part of the coven, the council that governed it, or either faction that had the capacity to expose our kind to the world with their tomfoolery.

My full name is Raven Lattice Marigold, and I'd become quite fond of this new way of life as a witch. In fact, I'm growing rather fond of my gift, and I was getting better at casting spells by the day.

Debatable, by even the loosest definition of the concept.

Okay. I'll admit that it had been a bit more trial and error than a complete success, but I hadn't sent the town into a tizzy or caused Leo to lose feeling in his tail for close to two months.

I'd call that a win.

Your abilities leave a lot to be desired.

Anyway, long story short, my mother had made a very valiant effort toward keeping this part of my lineage a secret... even from me. Regina Lattice Marigold had moved all the way to New York City and raised me there in hopes that I would have a normal life away from all of this.

It didn't quite work out the way she'd intended.

My grandmother, Rosemary Lattice Marigold, had dropped dead of a heart attack on her daily walk with Leo last summer. I'd basically inherited everything—the tea shop, the eerie little cottage on the edge of town, what you might call a wax golem who lived in a shed out back, and my de facto familiar—Leo.

Mr. Leo. You always leave my proper title off when introducing me.

I'd come to find out that a familiar almost always crossed into the afterlife with his or her charge, but Nan had committed a rather big no-no in the supernatural realm. She'd dabbled in black magic so that Leo could stay behind to help me acclimate to my newly inherited and previously unknown powers. Her intentions had been pure, but that hadn't prevented the consequences of her actions from leaving their mark on Leo and my life.

Get it over with. The readers should know that there are penalties for puttering around with the dark elements.

Oh, there had definitely been consequences. The residents just assumed that I'd rescued a homeless orange and black kittycat from a horrible life of scavenging food on the streets.

They didn't know that he was smart, witty, and compassionate underneath that rather disheveled exterior.

Now don't go ruining my reputation, Raven.

Alas, Leo had been left with a crooked tail, bent whiskers, tufts of hair that resembled dreadlocks, and a left eye that bulged out farther than his right when he was under stress. He was also a bit overweight, had short legs, and had a bit of a memory problem that popped up at the most inconvenient times, both of which he swore had improved with his overindulgent consumption of catnip. He certainly was a sight, but I'd be completely lost without him.

You make me sound like a mangy dog. I resent the inference.

"I'm thinking it's time to let this warlock thing go," Heidi advised, pointing her bag of nuts toward Rye, who was already cleaning up the brochures from his table. "He's a hardworking handyman trying to make a living. Don't you think that if he were part of your former coven, he would have made himself known already? You moved to town over six months ago."

"I guess." I was reluctant to admit that Heidi might be right, but as much as Leo had a habit of consuming too much catnip on a regular basis, he'd never hallucinated anything before. "Without any supporting evidence for our theory, it might be best to let it go for now."

Was I making the right decision? Heidi had a point. Rye had done nothing, with the exception of what Leo might or might not have seen, to indicate that he was anything other than an obscure member of the local society. Even if he was a warlock, didn't it stand to reason that he might be like me—someone with magical powers who wanted to be left in peace?

That might be all well and fine if the coven wasn't on the brink of war.

Leave it to Leo to put more doubts into my head.

You're welcome.

"I'll help you clean up, and then we can take this stuff back to the tea shop before hitting the carnival, maybe getting a cold beer, and listening to some outdoor folk music." Heidi carefully laid the paper cone on her chair after folding it closed, ensuring that none of the delicious contents fell to the ground. "Are we still on for looking at houses tomorrow? I can't wait to see the one that's on a corner lot with fruit trees in the backyard."

"Absolutely," I replied enthusiastically, turning off the base station that I'd used to plug in the line of urns to keep the samples hot for the tourists. It had been a great investment, and I'd been able to use the electric decanters, as well. I wish it was just that easy to flick a switch in order to turn off my suspicions of Rye. "I wouldn't miss it for the world. How many addresses are on the list?"

I'll be joining the two of you. I have to make sure there's a good window I can lounge in during my visits, preferably one with a tree so that I can continue to monitor the comings and goings of those pesky squirrels. They remind me of fairies, you know. Tricky little devils, always scheming over something or other.

To say that Leo and I were equally ecstatic over having my best friend move from New York City to Paramour Bay was an understatement. Don't get me wrong, I had no regrets about uprooting my life from the city. It had been hands down one of the best decisions I'd ever been forced to make, but there was nothing wrong with having a bit of icing with my cake.

I like my cake with a bit of fresh cream poured over the top.

Besides, I'd missed our wine nights and girl talk.

I only had to wait until the end of the month. That's when Heidi would be taking over the financial firm slash tax consultancy here in town from an older gentleman by the name of Beetle, who was retiring. He'd gotten the nickname from driving around in his old red Volkswagen bug. On a side note and for future reference, he resembled the mad scientist from *Back to the Future*.

Do you think my BFF owns a comb?

Beetle also happened to be my part-time employee, not wanting to become stagnant during his budding retirement. He was also the prime supplier of Leo's catnip addiction, which was the only reason the older gentleman had become Leo's best friend forever.

It hadn't been too hard to keep my secret of being a witch under wraps, especially considering that I had followed in Nan's footsteps by creating holistic tea blends for my customers' various ailments. Neither Beetle nor my clients were aware of the magical touch I sprinkled over their orders, and it needed to stay that way.

Anyway, not too much damage had been done during Beetle's training. I had to keep reminding myself that it was only for a few hours a day. He wasn't cut out for the retail business. On the plus side, he was great at keeping my books in order.

"Not a lot of houses are for sale, so there are only three to look at tomorrow and one on Sunday before I head back to the city." Heidi had efficiently cleared away the sample cups and tossed the ones that had been used into a nearby trash can. The only thing left to do was to empty the carafes and place them back into the box, along with the base station. Unfortunately, Leo was currently occupying said box. I was going to have to evict him before we could return everything to the tea shop on my handy cart. I'd already loaded up the various tea implements and coffee machine into a second box behind my chair. "If I don't find a house I like in the adjacent neighborhood, I could always look at the waterfront properties. They're just so expensive, and I was looking forward to reducing my housing costs after living in the city."

I had no doubt that Heidi had tucked away a few pennies here and there for such an occasion. She'd majored in finance and had gone to work right out of college at one of the most prestigious accounting firms in New York City. Granted, the cost of living there versus here was a major difference, but Heidi had always dreamed of owning her own firm. She'd been saving her spare change to make that dream happen since way back in high school.

With the deal she'd made with her company in the city, she would be able to give her clients better service with little upfront capital outlay. It was a win-win for everyone involved, and I'm sure it also kept a few dollars in the bank as a down payment so that she could find the perfect place to live.

"We'll find you the right home," I reassured her with a smile. "I promise."

One of the puffy clouds shifted above us to allow more rays of sunshine to brighten the late afternoon. I took that as a sign of happier times to come. Heidi was right about forgetting this warlock stuff. Surely Rye would have said or done something by now that would have confirmed my suspicions.

Aren't you always warning me about tempting fate?

"I'm not tempting anything. I'm packing up our booth," I explained, shooing Leo out of the cardboard box. He was reluctant to give up such a good spot where he could keep an eye on the squirrels, but I didn't give him much of a choice. "It's been over eight weeks, and we've done nothing but stress over the situation. I'm officially claiming that you hallucinated...you know...after consuming too much catnip. Let's forget it ever happened."

"That's the spirit," Heidi chimed in, used to me talking to Leo. She grabbed a few of the miscellaneous items off the table that still needed to be packed away and made her way around the back of the chairs to our cart. "Jack just texted me. He's going to park near the tea shop, so why don't I take these boxes back with me? I'll tell Beetle that it's okay to close up, and then we'll all meet you back here in around twenty minutes."

Heidi had begun dating a local state police detective a few months ago. He was the first steady relationship that she'd had in quite a while, and it was one that I think could go the distance.

I don't know about that. Hey, maybe those squirrels can come in handy, after all.

Let's just say that Leo wasn't too thrilled with Heidi dating Detective Jack Swanson, because no one could dare be good enough to date his beloved Heidi. I understood where he was coming from because I only wanted the best for her, too.

"That sounds good," I replied before fishing my keys out of my purse. I'd switched to one that was technically the size of a tote bag, but it worked given today's event. "Beetle is better at closing out the store than I am. You know, seeing as he's not that good at the sales part of the job, I might have him switch his hours so that he can close every evening and tally the receipts."

"Since I'm handling the shop's taxes, it would be nice to see a little organization in your bookkeeping." Heidi was smiling as she stacked the two boxes on the small fold-up cart I'd found in the storage room of the tea shop. I sighed a little in disappointment when she suddenly remembered to snag the paper cone of candied almonds off the chair. "There isn't a chance I'm leaving these behind, girlfriend, especially when I know Leo probably already has a plan to use them in order to lure those squirrels down from the tree."

She knows me far too well.

"Thanks for taking this stuff back for me. How about I meet the two of you at the pizza stand?"

I handed Heidi my spare set of keys before scanning the crowd, hoping to catch a glimpse of Liam. I'd say three-quarters of the festival were residents of Paramour Bay, but the small traveling carnival had made quite the attraction and brought in quite a few tourists and residents of other nearby towns. It would be almost impossible to locate him in these crowds. I debated on whether or not to text him, but he'd mentioned earlier this morning that he'd hoped to take a small break for dinner with Jack, Heidi, and me.

So...you're saying I'm on my own for dinner? What? You expect me to root through the garbage cans for sustenance? Like a raccoon?

Ted—the wax golem-like figure I'd mentioned earlier—had assured me that he'd feed Leo his favorite evening meal. I'd already made arrangements with him because I wasn't sure how long Heidi and I would be out this evening. She was staying with me until she returned to the city on Sunday evening. Seeing as Leo could read my thoughts, I didn't have to say anything aloud for someone to overhear me and think I was losing a grip on my sanity.

You had a grip?

I once again focused on the faces in the crowd. Otis and Karen were walking down the middle of the now mostly empty tables that would be taken down one by one by the hired festival workers. I gave the former sheriff and his wife a quick wave before going back to scanning the numerous faces.

Unfortunately, not one of them was the man I was looking for.

I crossed the street and blended in with the crowd, holding my wristband up to show the lady at the gate that I was allowed free access to the carnival as one of the local vendors. It had been an added benefit to leasing a booth for the afternoon. She smiled and waved me through.

There was something to be said about the noises and competitive shouts coming from the numerous attractions that held various games, from popping balloons to tossing rings. Laughter and hollering rang out from the players, while the carnival barkers did their best to coax more onlookers to join in the games.

Maybe Liam was already near the food stands, given that it was around dinnertime, and that's where the majority of the crowd would be gathered. I debated taking the long way around, which would have led me through the twirling rides and a small rollercoaster for the really young attendees, but it would be quicker for me to cut in between the kissing booth and the dunk tank. Neither booth was currently occupied, but both sported a sign that the fun began at six o'clock with various members of the town's elite.

I was grateful I'd brought a light sweater with me today. The weather during this time of year could be unpredictable once the sun went down, and the leftover chill from the cold season seemed to linger around in the later part of the evenings. One of the gathering clouds must have glided in the sun's path, and I had to suppress a shiver when the shade began to cascade over me ever so slowly.

I stepped over a small hole in the ground, beginning my trek that would save me much-needed time. The delicious aroma of funnel cakes and popcorn drifted toward me on the light breeze, which was most likely why I'd focused my attention ahead of me. Unfortunately, removing my gaze from where I was walking prompted my accident-prone tendencies to spring into action.

There was nothing I could do when I tripped over...a pair of worn black boots?

I'd caught sight of them as I reached my hands out to cushion my fall.

"I'm so sorry," I immediately claimed, managing to catch myself from stumbling even farther. I wiped my hands together to get any remaining dirt off my palms, wondering what the man could be working on that had him lying on the ground at such an odd angle. It was then that I noticed the tingling sensation in the middle of my right palm. "I was just trying to take a shortcut through..."

My words eventually trailed off when I realized that the legs attached to those boots weren't moving at all.

Literally, there was no movement from the body.

My throat instantly closed when I realized the tingling in my hand had nothing to do with my close collision with the ground, and everything to do with the fact that the earth had been trying to warn me that something was out of balance.

Hey, Raven. We need to talk about Ted. He had the audacity to try to feed me those leftovers in the—

Leo had suddenly materialized next to me, and I didn't have to look down at him to know that his left eye was bulging a bit more than usual. I understood his disbelief all too well, because I still hadn't been able to swallow. As a matter of fact, I'm pretty sure the waves of contractions in my throat were going in the opposite direction.

Please tell me that isn't a body. Let me clarify—please tell me that isn't a dead body.

I wish I could reassure Leo that he was hallucinating again, but I was still having a bit of trouble keeping those candied almonds where I'd put them. Quite frankly, I was starting to really doubt that Leo had hallucinated anything.

I suddenly feel a hairball trying to come up.

You see, the man lying dead behind the kissing booth was none other than the same carnival worker whom I had seen talking with Rye Dolgiram not an hour ago. As a matter of fact, the dead man was still clutching Rye's brochure in his hand.

Two

"Raven, I can't believe this happened again," Heidi murmured, scooting closer to me on one of the picnic tables so we could conserve some heat. Darkness had fallen, but several bright klieg lights had been set up all around the grounds of the carnival to advertise the nighttime festivities. Inside the carnival, long lines of Edison bulbs surrounded each attraction, and colorful strings of multicolored Chinese lanterns had been strung between all the booths and the food trailers. No one could have anticipated that a murder would take place here, and now the area was deathly quiet. "What are the odds that you stumbled across two bodies in the span of six months?"

The odds are next to zero, but that didn't stop it from happening again. I should have known that history was bound to repeat itself with Barney Fife guarding the festivities. It's like we're stuck in that one movie where that blonde gal has to relive her birthday over every single day. It's a vicious time loop we can't get out of, and no amount of catnip can make it any better.

Leo remained invisible to those around us, but I could only imagine that he was pacing back and forth in worry at our feet.

Of course, he was exaggerating. Well, not about the history part, and it had nothing to do with the security Liam provided the town. You see, on the very first day that I arrived in Paramour Bay, Heidi and I found a dead body in the back of the tea shop. The victim had turned out to be a total stranger to everyone in town.

The man's death had been the first murder to happen in Paramour Bay for over fifty-three years. So yes, my arrival had caught the attention of the local residents. With that said, the case had been solved, and life here in our wonderful small town had returned to normal.

I think you're some kind of weird magnet for death and bad karma.

"Heidi, this particular dead guy was the same man who was talking to Rye when you were standing in line for those candied almonds," I whispered, not wanting Liam or anyone else to overhear me. I'd eventually tell him, but I also had to worry about the ramifications of such a disclosure. What if Rye actually *was* a warlock? What if he'd used his magic to attack and kill someone? I couldn't very well explain that to Liam, which meant Leo and I would have to do some investigating of our own. "We need to find out how the man died, just in case it's linked back to the coven and witchcraft."

That was so not what I was thinking. I have a better idea. What if we let good ol' sheriff Liam do his job for once? It's good to be seen as a productive member of society, especially if you're the one filling a position in an elected office.

"I'm sure Liam or Jack will be over this way soon with more information." Heidi hadn't brought a jacket with her, so she was wearing one of Jack's state police windbreakers. She pulled the black nylon material around her shoulders a little tighter, never taking her worried gaze off the two men as they did their duty. They were currently talking with the county medical examiner while two members of her staff zipped up the body bag. "Maybe we have nothing to worry about, and the man died of a massive heart attack."

Heidi's got the right idea. We shouldn't assume the worst. For all we know, it was those darn pesky squirrels involved in a massive conspiracy to assassinate a man for his role in ridding the East Coast of furry-tailed rats.

Squirrels had nothing to do with the carnival worker's death. As much as Leo was attempting to get my mind off the fact that I'd somehow ended up tripping over another dead body, I was pretty sure this was fate's way of saying we needed to get involved.

Where are you getting this stuff? Do you have a crystal ball that I'm not aware of, or are you receiving coded signals from space aliens over your fillings? I'm pretty sure that fate doesn't want me to do anything. Well, maybe to go home and spark up a fresh pipe of premium catnip. Good ol' fate...she's got her own things to worry about. If you're referring to our reputation in the afterlife as paranormal amateur sleuths, I'll have you know that no one ever lives up to their afterlife reputation. No one. Literally. Do you know why? Because we all die in the end, just like that poor carnival worker—a man who by chance choked to death on a random flying acorn he just happened to accidentally ingest while his mouth was hanging open as he walked under a tree filled with squirrels. I, for one, can't afford to die a squirrel-related death and leave you here all alone. Could you imagine the trouble you would get into without me here to warn you off? Not to mention the wrath of my beloved Rosemary, who's probably still trying to find a ticket back here to find out why I'm slacking in my duties by trying to teach you how to cast the most basic spells without setting fire to the entire town. Little does she understand that you're impossible to mentor.

"The man was probably in his forties," I pointed out softly, wrapping my arms tight around my waist as Leo carried on with one of his tangents. Due to the carnival being shut down for the rest of the evening, the only people left behind were those who were colleagues and friends of the victim, along with a few of us witnesses. They all seemed to be in shock, and I was right there with them. Well, except for the clown. Those jesters never seemed quite right. The smile on his face was kind of creepy. "I don't think he died from natural causes. My right palm was tingling when I tripped over his legs. I sensed danger."

Being a witch, I had been given the amazing gift of sensing when something was amiss. The warmth usually began in the center of my palm, allowing my body to draw in the energy the earth provided me for a sense of self-protection. I was still somewhat new to all of this, but I was learning more each day.

Raven, you tripped over a dead body. Your palm should have been shooting off fire bolts, not tingling from lack of circulation. Let's face it. You're a bit defective.

Leo wasn't going to like my theory as to why I hadn't been forewarned when I'd stumbled upon the body, so I purposefully continued to watch the scene unfold in front of me. With the town of Paramour Bay being so small, Liam usually handed off the felony cases to the state police. Enter Detective Jack Swanson, who thankfully had already been on the scene due to Heidi's attendance. He'd been able to call in forensics, the medical examiner, as well as additional officers who could help take statements.

What harebrained theory are you talking about?

"Let's just wait to decide on anything until Liam or Jack

tells us how the man died," Heidi said, bouncing her knee up and down in worry. "If his death was due to natural causes, then there's nothing to be done."

Let's get back to this critical theory of yours.

"Beetle wanted me to let you know that he'll work all day at the tea shop tomorrow, seeing as it's Saturday. My morning with him today was productive, so we were able to file a lot of his clients' taxes." Heidi was doing her best to keep my mind off the chaotic scene in front of us. "I say we sleep in and have a late breakfast with huge piles of bacon. Oh, and loads of coffee. Then we can look at some of those houses on my list and make a girl's day of it. What do you say?"

Count me in if there's catnip involved, and we'll leave this investigation in the hands of the true professionals. If we do that, you don't have to tell me about any of those theories you have rattling around in that head of yours. Sound like a plan?

I was prevented from answering Heidi when Liam began to walk our way. He was rubbing the back of his neck, which told me all I needed to know. We'd been dating since New Year's Eve. I'd gotten to know some of his tells, and his neck rub told me that he had bad news.

What's to say he doesn't have a pulled muscle from riding the kiddie rollercoaster one too many times? Sure, it's all fun and games until you need a chiropractor the next day. You always assume the worst.

I actually considered myself an optimist. Unfortunately, tripping over a dead body had the strange effect of being shot with a syringe full of realism.

I hate shots. Now that I think about it, shots rank right up there with my phobia of spiders, the international squirrel conspiracy...and clowns. Did that red-nosed crayon eater just take a step toward us?

"How are you holding up?" Liam asked gently, stroking my arm with concern.

Not good now that I'm thinking about that clown. He's staring at me, and I'm not even visible. Raven, make him stop. You don't think he's in league with those darn squirrels, do you? I bet he smells of acorns.

"Raven would be better if you told us that the man died of a heart attack," Heidi interjected, looking up at Liam with a half-smile and false hope. Leo's comment had me glancing over at the clown, who did seem as if he'd come a bit closer to the picnic table than he had before. "I would be, too."

I'm going to take a walk...far away from that clown and that half-baked theory you think you came up with in the last few hours.

"I wish I could." Liam thinned his lips and shook his head in regret. "The victim's name was Kevin Paul. He was one of the carnival's new additions for the season. From some of the preliminary statements, the carnies don't know too much about him other than he joined them on their last stop and that he mostly keeps to himself."

Heidi's blue eyes glanced my way as if she were waiting for me to come clean about Kevin Paul visiting Rye's vendor table. It wasn't like I'd been the only other business owner out front, though. Numerous people had seen the two conversing at the table, and I didn't want to be the one to bring it to Liam's attention just in case magic had been the motive.

"How did Mr. Paul die?" I asked before holding my breath in anticipation while waiting for Liam to answer.

"The victim had a pretty severe contusion on the back of his head. The medical examiner won't give a definite cause of death until after the autopsy, but I think it's safe to assume someone attacked him from the rear. The way he was lying on the ground when you found him suggests he didn't accidentally trip and fall backward. Raven, did Mr. Paul stop by your table today?"

I was so engrossed in what Liam had to say that I didn't have time to consider my answer. The words just poured out of my mouth like a flood.

"No, but I saw him talking with Rye Dolgiram this afternoon. He gave Mr. Paul one of his brochures."

I was such a horrible liar, I couldn't even tell the truth convincingly. It was a wonder I hadn't blurted out everything else, and I hated that doubt to keep my secret crept in and shook my confidence.

"We found a fistful of brochures from the vendors in Mr. Paul's back pocket and one in his hand." Liam might have been talking to Heidi and me, but his gaze was constantly scanning our surroundings. I followed his lead, picking up on a few things myself...such as the clown had disappeared while I was distracted. "I'll talk to Rye and the others to see if the victim was acting strange prior to his demise. I find it odd that he was visiting the vendor tables when he should have been working the rides he'd been assigned to this afternoon. Listen, are you and Heidi okay to make it home alone? It's going to be a long night, and the two of you don't need to sit out here in the cold waiting for us."

"We'll be fine," Heidi assured Liam with a smile, nudging my knee so that I agreed. "Right?"

"Yes, yes, of course," I replied, squeezing Liam's hand in reassurance so that he wouldn't worry. "We'll be fine. Will you call me later if you have a chance?"

"That I can do." Liam surprised me by leaning forward and pressing a tender kiss to my cheek. He'd done so in the past, but he was usually very careful not to show public displays of affection when he was on duty. Granted, Jack was now here and had assumed lead on the murder investigation, but Liam would work the case alongside his friend. "Try and get some sleep. If you need anything, give me a call. I can be out there in one twitch of a squirrel's tail."

Liam didn't immediately walk back to where Jack and the medical examiner were still talking. Instead, he joined a small group of carnival workers who were standing off to the side. The fact that he was wearing a pair of jeans and worn cowboy boots seemed to put the others at ease. He wasn't even wearing the usual khaki dress shirt that he considered his official police uniform. Instead, he was wearing a black dress shirt with the sleeves rolled up just below his elbows.

"I know that look," Heidi interjected, standing up from her seat on the bench and standing in front of me to block my view. She tucked some of those blonde strands behind her ear when a gentle breeze snuck in between the game stands. "I'm usually the first one to jump headfirst into these things, but we need to take a step back and really think about this now that Rye could be involved. Can't you do your..."

Heidi wiggled her fingers, indicating she was talking about magical divination.

"You know me too well," I murmured, going through my mind the various spells that could possibly help us in this situation. "I need some small object that belonged to the victim."

Heidi arched one of her brows, telling me pretty much what I already knew—that was going to be impossible to do while the police were investigating the crime scene.

"How do you feel about us coming back to the carnival tomorrow, in between looking at those three houses?" I'd come up with a plan. If it worked, we'd have answers by tomorrow night. "We can play a few games, ride the Ferris wheel, and maybe even get our fortunes told by Madam Solaris as an added bonus."

Heidi understood everything I was suggesting, which was to talk to as many carnival employees—or carnies, as Liam had called them—as we could in order to locate something of Mr. Paul's that I could use in a scry spell. The incantations that I'd managed to cast successfully were easier for me to perform than the ones I'd never tried before, and the last thing any of us needed was another spell gone awry.

Not to get sidetracked, but my last spell was basically me shooting some of Cupid's arrows at random townsfolk. It hadn't been pretty. People had been running off together behind the bushes.

"The campers of the employees are parked out near the back field, but I'm not sure how you think we'll get access to Kevin Paul's personal belongings."

"We might not need to," I explained as we both began walking toward the exit. "I overheard one of the carnies say that Mr. Paul worked the tilt-a-whirl. Maybe he left behind something that I could use, such as a water bottle or a shop rag. Most of the male workers seem to have one stuffed in their back pockets to wipe grease off their hands."

"I like the way you think," Heidi praised, linking her arm into mine as we finally hit Oceanview Drive. "One thing I can say with some certainty is that life in this small coastal town won't be boring considering the increased crime rate since your arrival."

After the last eight weeks of constantly worrying that Rye was some type of warlock, boring actually sounded kind of nice. Unfortunately, we now had a murder mystery to solve.

I was usually against calling my mother when things began to go sideways, but she definitely had more knowledge than I did about the coven. With that said, I knew someone who might have the information I sought regarding Rye Dolgiram. One simple phone call was all that was needed in order to find out if he'd ever been part of the coven.

Did I really want to play that card?

Was it worth contacting my great-aunt, who'd all but cut my grandmother out of her life all those years ago when the coven had excommunicated my Nan?

Just the thought of opening that door made me a bit queasy.

Not as queasy as what I'm about to tell you.

"Leo, where have you been?" Heidi asked, catching sight of my familiar as he came galloping across the street to where we were on the sidewalk. She leaned down when he plopped himself in front of us, almost completely out of breath. "Oh, you poor boy. Here. Let me carry you."

Heidi hoisted Leo up into her arms, which was no easy feat considering his weight issues. With that said, he'd stopped talking to rub his chin against hers. The two of them started forward, leaving me to hang back while waiting for the bomb to drop.

Again, there was nothing but the sound of Heidi's affectionate murmurs and what I'm pretty sure was purring loud enough to cause any squirrels still awake to take notice.

"Leo," I called out harshly, quickly marching forward to catch up with them. "Leo, you can't say something like that and then pretend you didn't. What did you find out?"

What did I say?

"You said—"

Ohhhh, right back there. Scratch a little more to the left. That's right. Doesn't Heidi give the best scratches?

"What are you two carrying on about now?" Heidi asked,

still running her fingernails back and forth underneath Leo's chin. She even planted a kiss on top of his head. "The poor thing is out of breath. Were you chasing those nasty squirrels?"

"Leo said that something he found out while he was near the crime scene would make me upset to my stomach," I relayed, going back through what could only be called a one-sided conversation. "Then his short-term memory loss kicked in, and now I don't know what he meant."

"Any crime scene would make us sick to our stomachs," Heidi pointed out, shifting Leo's weight so that he was easier to carry. "Leo, why did you go over there anyway?"

Whatever you do, don't tell her that I'm scared of clowns. The fact that she knows about my arachnophobia is bad enough. I'm pretty sure we both have the same view when it comes to squirrels, though.

I had to remind myself that Leo's faulty memory was a consequence of Nan's brief dabble in the dark elements. He wasn't to blame, and I needed to have a bit more patience and understanding at times like these.

"Leo, you went for a walk when Liam came to talk to me," I reminded him, hoping to jog his memory. "Remember?"

Vaguely.

We'd walked the stretch of Oceanview Drive and were now at the intersection of River Bay, the main thoroughfare through town. My beat-up old Corolla was parked in front of my tea shop, so we crossed the street in no hurry since there was currently no traffic. Technically, the vacated sidewalks this time of night made Paramour Bay seem like a ghost town.

Don't say that word. You're liable to send a signal to the afterlife and attract something.

Well, maybe that was why the hairs on the back of my neck were standing at attention, and the center of my palm began to tingle. As a matter of fact, a bit of warmth had invaded my fingers.

I looked down Oceanview Drive, but I didn't see a thing except the lighted entrance of the carnival. Why did it feel as if someone was watching us?

Someone's watching us? Where?

Heidi was a few steps ahead of me. I'd slowed down to try and take a look around us, but again, I didn't see anything out of the ordinary. Leo had popped his head over Heidi's shoulder, his green eyes slanting at the insinuation we weren't alone.

Is it that clown or the squirrels? It's that red-nosed crayon eater, isn't it?

"Why do you say that, Leo?" I asked, prompting Heidi to stop in her tracks so that I could catch up with them. "Did you see the clown when you went for a walk around the carnival grounds?"

"Clown?" Heidi asked with a frown, clearly not liking the funny-faced carnival attraction, either.

Do you really think that I would have taken myself anywhere near that horror show in pantaloons? What kind of mentally defective nutbag came up with the idea of putting an orange wig, a red nose, and a painted evil smile on someone and thinking children would find them funny? I've seen the It *movie. I know what happens when a clown crawls out from a sewage drain, and it ain't pretty.*

I was getting nowhere with trying to get Leo to remember what he'd wanted to tell me, so I sighed in resignation as we continued to walk to my car in silence. At least the tingling and warmth in my hand had started to subside.

"We'll get you home and feed you dinner," Heidi told Leo as she continued to scratch behind his ears. "Then we'll snuggle by the fire."

Home.

Leo sighed in contentment and then rested his cheek against Heidi's shoulder.

I'm going to love having her here on a full-time basis. It's going to be so much—

I'd had the keys in my hand that Heidi had returned to me when Leo's head lifted up faster than those squirrels had vacated the carnival area upon hearing all the commotion.

Oh, this isn't good. This is bad. Really bad.

"What is it?" Heidi whispered, knowing full well that Leo was talking to me from the way I'd stopped in my tracks. "Did Leo find out that Rye killed Kevin Paul?"

It's certainly looking that way. Raven, we need to call in reinforcements. This is an all-hands-on-deck situation, and that includes—I can't believe I'm saying this—your mother.

"Why?" I asked, bracing myself for Leo's answer.

In hindsight, I should have leaned against the car for added leverage.

I overheard the good ol' detective tell the medical examiner that the address on Kevin Paul's driver's license is none other than…Windsor.

Windsor, Connecticut—the very town in which my family's coven was located, and the one that was on the verge of a war fought with witchcraft.

Three

⁓

"Raven. My dear, Raven. You have no worries. I've got the day covered," Beetle reassured me with a pat on the back as he walked past me toward the cash register. The tips of his white hair floated behind him, similar to the way the threads of an angora sweater would when outside in the gentle breeze. "Leo has his catnip, the shelves are completely stocked, and there are no new sales items that I need to worry about coding into the register. No, siree. No worries here at all."

Beetle had on his usual grey cardigan sweater and colorful tie, this one a bright purple. He had a tendency to say something twice, but I'd become used to it by now. It was rather endearing.

What I wasn't used to was leaving the tea shop all day in the hands of someone so...eccentric. Now that I looked back on the six months I'd been in Paramour Bay, I'd never let anyone take over for an entire day. What if I came back and found that Beetle had turned the tea shop into some type of geriatric time machine?

On second thought, that might not be such a bad idea.

I'd give almost anything to go back to last night before I tripped over that dead body. Then again, why only go back to last night? It would be even better to go back eight weeks and somehow have Leo *not* witness Rye use magic on my gate.

There is still a chance that I could have hallucinated the entire thing. Slim. Well, a little less than slim, but that still constitutes a chance, however slight. Right?

Leo had consumed his all-time favorite treat on his plush pillow in the display window and was now lying on his back with his short legs straight up in the air, allowing the morning rays of sunshine to warm his belly. His concerns seemed to have mellowed with each lick of the minty herb, so it wouldn't be in my best interest to trust his somewhat skewed judgment at the moment.

Such high standards.

"Beetle, please make sure to provide Candy with those holistic tea blends I made for her customers at the hair salon," I reminded him, wishing I wasn't so nervous about leaving Beetle in charge of the shop. Granted, he'd come a long way in the past eight weeks, but I still had trouble delegating responsibilities. "Oh, and Pearl mentioned that she might stop by for that diffuser she ordered. It's on the top shelf in the storage room. There is even a tag attached with her name on it."

"I've got this taken care of," Beetle reassured me, pulling the stool up closer to the counter. He patted the hard surface twice in a display of confidence. "You two go on ahead and find our dear Heidi a nice home to roost in."

Roost, Heidi mouthed with a shocked expression. Eventually, she smiled at the old saying. She even pretended to flap her arms like a chicken, but I was too worked up to find her amusing with my current level of anxiety.

Leo sounded as if he were choking on a hairball, but I'd

gotten used to the sound of his laughter. He certainly was enjoying himself over there.

My BFF never fails to entertain.

"We're actually waiting for my mother, so now would be a good time to ask me anything you think might be a problem while I'm gone." I glanced out the display window, but Regina was nowhere in sight. I'd called her on the advice of both Heidi and Leo, and my mother's reaction had been what I'd expected —a long, drawn-out silence that had me asking twice if she'd still been on the line. "Mom should be here any minute."

Oh, joy. Remind me again why I said calling her would be a good idea? Had I consumed too much catnip? I don't believe I would have made such a suggestion otherwise.

Heidi was busy brewing up a pot of coffee, most of which we would drink before leaving for breakfast, and the other half would be used as samples for the morning customers. We had a plan in place, and a good one if you ask me.

Oh, that's right. The dead guy just had to be from Windsor. Have I mentioned that you're a magnet for bad luck, Schleprock?

First, we'd get something to eat over at the diner so that we could be front and center for any scuttlebutt making the rounds regarding last night's murder. I could see the place was already crowded with the staff from the carnival, the tourists who were in town for the festival, and the usual patrons who always started their weekend with a meal at the diner.

I'm staying here with my BFF. Call me when you...no. I take that back. You and your mother can handle this one on your own, because I'm going to take a well-deserved staycation day. Most cats don't have to put up with this much bother, you know.

Afterward, I'd stop in at the station to see Liam, where in all likelihood Jack would be investigating this case. Heidi and I would attempt to see if any new information had been uncovered since last night and continue to hope that any such evidence didn't point toward Rye.

Once the carnival opened its gates at eleven o'clock, we would then begin our search for an object owned by the deceased. Once we had something of substance in hand, my mother and I would be able to cast a spell that would give us an indication of what happened during the last few moments before Kevin Paul was murdered.

If magic was involved and we discovered that Rye really was a warlock who'd used his powers in the worst way imaginable, we'd have no choice but to put in a call to Aunt Rowena. Granted, we wanted nothing to do with her and whatever war was brewing between the two factions of the coven, but any type of situation that involved a wayward warlock warranted intervention from the council.

Oh, and Heidi still had to tour three houses.

Perfect. You, Heidi, and Regina have things well in hand. The day is starting to look up, and it's not even nine o'clock. I love my morning wake and bake.

"Regina is visiting this weekend?" Beetle asked, perking up quite a bit. I wasn't sure why he would be happy that my mom was coming to town, but Beetle had always been a bit of a strange bird. "Isn't this just dandy? Raven, how does this tie look with my sweater? Oh, this is just dandy, indeed."

I exchanged quizzical glances with Heidi.

Raven, my good mood is quickly evaporating. You're polluting my karma.

I guess I had never thought about it, but Beetle and my mother were around the same age, minus about five years. Considering Mom hadn't moved to New York City until her early twenties, chances are that the two of them had gone to school together. It wasn't like Paramour Bay had a large school system.

I'd rather skip this little trip down memory lane. Didn't you mention that we have a murder mystery to solve? I guess there is no need for me to take a staycation day when things are just starting to come together. Shall we head out?

For Leo to want to dive headfirst into a murder investigation over talking about the past told me there was a lot to be gleaned from this conversation he would rather avoid taking place. Unfortunately, I wasn't so sure I actually wanted to hear a recount of my mother's past love life.

You don't. Trust me.

"Beetle, you're from Paramour Bay originally, right?" I asked, prodding him to open up about his connection with the Marigold family. "Were you ever friends with my mother?"

Look at the time. We should head on out now, don't you think? The weather could turn. It's happened before.

Leo had rolled over and stood on all four paws, telling me he was quite serious about avoiding this conversation. It was hard to miss the disdainful glance he gave at the lipstick stain left from a fairy we had saved on a past case before arching his back to stretch. His bad mood had just gotten worse, regardless of his morning treat.

Fairies. You just had to remind me. Listen, what time did you say the carnival opened? We should start walking that way, or we'll miss the scuttlebutt at the diner. Your mother can catch up with us when she arrives in town. I'm sure she wouldn't have much trouble finding us.

There was no way I was missing out on this conversation, especially when Leo was so dead set against it.

"Why, yes, I am from Paramour Bay. I was born and raised here, my dear Raven." Beetle had stood from the stool behind him, standing up straight and fiddling with his tie to make sure that it was tucked securely inside his cardigan sweater. "This is a wonderful town, Raven. Wonderful. I was quite sad when your mother decided to move away. I haven't seen her in many, many years."

Looking back over the times my mother had been in town, she had always missed seeing Beetle. With that said, she'd never really mentioned much of anything about which residents she'd known on a personal level. Other than Cora Barnes, who was pretty much my mother's high school nemesis, the only other person my mom had exchanged more than a passing hello with was Trixie. Cora owned the malt shop next door, and Trixie owned the diner. Just who else had my mother been friends with that I didn't know about?

Didn't you say that we needed to find an item owned by the victim? What was his name? Oh, that's right—Kevin Paul. That poor, poor man. He deserves justice, Raven. No time to waste. Chop, chop!

Leo was starting to give me a headache.

"Were you and Regina friends when you both were younger?" Heidi asked, sealing the two cups with disposable lids in such a natural way that Beetle had no idea she was fishing for information. Her train of thought was on the same track as mine, and I focused my full attention on my employee. How could I have not seen what a wealth of information he could be regarding my mother's childhood? "Did the two of you go to high school together?"

Both Heidi and Beetle ignored Leo's loud meows, both having grown used to his bid for attention. Of course, only Heidi was aware that Leo was talking to me and clearly showing his displeasure. Well, Leo could keep meowing until the cows came home.

Fine. I'll cut to the chase. Trust me when I say that you don't want to know about your mother's past love interests. She chose to leave Paramour Bay in her early twenties, and that's that. End of story. Nothing more to say.

"We did, we did go to high school together," Beetle answered in his usual fashion. He leaned back on his dress shoes, a faraway look in his eyes as memories from the past obviously resurfaced. "Regina was such a beautiful young woman, always walking around with a glint of mischief in those green eyes of hers. I recall asking her to the senior prom and having my heart broken into tiny pieces when she said she hadn't planned on going. You see, she was a freshman."

Hearing about how my mother broke Beetle's heart confirmed Leo's outlook about the past, but maybe Leo was right. We had a lot on our plate, and I was beginning to think that now wasn't the time or place to hear about my mother's past deeds. A daughter needed to be in a certain mood to be given detailed information that was rather sensitive.

Besides, we had a murder mystery to solve.

That's the spirit. Hey, seeing as you're now all gung-ho about this amateur sleuthing business, what are the odds that I can still get that staycation?

I needed to signal Heidi that it was best we leave well enough alone. I couldn't wait for the infusion of caffeine either, so I walked over to the high-top table where Heidi had set our drinks. I gave her the cut-it-out motion before picking up my coffee.

"That's so sad, Beetle." Heidi had begun setting out some sample cups around the carafe, though she was still hanging on to Beetle's every word. She gave me a glance that said she didn't understand my hand chop signal, which did not bode well for me. "Did Regina end up going with someone else that year, or did she stay home?"

It's hard to believe that I love Heidi so much. Her inability to understand our cues is going to have all of us landing in hot water.

I had a feeling that Leo was talking about my biological father. Mom didn't have a lot of heart-to-heart conversations concerning the past, and I'd learned long ago not to ask questions she didn't want to answer. She'd become quite the expert at pretending that anything that happened before she moved to New York didn't exist, so you can imagine the shock she'd been dealt when she discovered that Nan had passed away and left everything for me to deal with.

It had occurred to me that my biological father might still reside in Paramour Bay, but then that thought had flown right out the window when my mother began visiting me on and off since my move here. Would she have put herself in the crosshairs of the very man who'd broken her heart?

Regina only comes to this town if it's to try to talk you into returning to New York City or to help clean up one of your messes. I, for one, would like to keep it that way.

"To this day, I don't believe Newt appreciated your mother's company. He was a couple of years older than her, too, but he wasn't a senior like me." Beetle had made that confession, followed by a tsking noise. He had no idea that he'd knocked all the oxygen out of my lungs. "Well, bygones are bygones, right? It will be such a pleasure to see her again. An absolute pleasure!"

Newt?

Paramour Bay's local mechanic?

What can of worms had I just popped open?

Between spiders, fairies, and clowns...I can't handle worms,

Raven. I'm now at my wits' end. You need to stop digging this hole we're all going to end up in...with those slimy worms.

Newt and my mother had dated in high school. This was news to me, and I'd had about all the history lessons I could stand for one day.

Considering I was the spitting image of the Marigold women with long black hair, practically iridescent green eyes, and high cheekbones, it would have been rather difficult to guess what my father would have looked like when he was younger, let alone what his appearance might be in his mid to late fifties.

Who said anything about Newt being your biological father? How in the supernatural realm did this beautiful morning get set on fire and turned into nothing but a pile of ash? This conversation might be worse than seeing that creepy clown from last night. Wait. I take that back. Clowns are spawned from the devil, so maybe you're skirting the line there.

Heidi had just finished pouring the last sample cup and placing it on the warmer when she finally caught on to what I'd been attempting to avoid. Of course, it helped that Leo had jumped down from the display window and was becoming rather hoarse from the frustrated meows. Her pink lips formed the perfect O as she grabbed her own cup of coffee and began moving toward the exit. Maybe our future cues should come in the form of a brick.

There might be something worse than clowns around here. If so, I'm sure it'll turn up sooner rather than later.

On that note, the bell above the door rang, and I didn't have to turn around to know that my mother had entered the tea shop. Leo had already given her an introduction, which she'd clearly heard from her sharp reply.

"Leo, it's always a distinct pleasure."

There was nothing unusual about my mother greeting Leo, especially seeing as he'd strolled closer to the glass door when he'd been in a panic over Beetle's history lesson. Beetle had no idea that my mother and I were witches, but humans talked to their pets all the time. It was only considered eccentric behavior, and it was rather cute to pretend that they could understand us.

Did you just infer that I'm a common housecat?

"Mom, I'm so glad you could come for the festival my first year representing the shop," I exclaimed, turning around with a forced smile. It would take a while for the weight of this morning's conversation to ease, but now wasn't the time for me to go digging into my mother's love life to discover who my biological father might be. "Heidi and I are starving. Let's walk over to the diner."

You can't throw the hammer and not expect it to hit something, Thor.

"My beautiful Regina, it's been way too long," Beetle exclaimed with happiness, making his way over to her as he held out both of his hands. It was a good thing Heidi had veered from the exit and joined me back at the high-top table, because it was her surprised reaction that told me I hadn't been mistaken when I saw a flush of red cover my mother's cheeks. "You haven't aged a bit, my dear. You look as stunning as ever. Just stunning!"

Beetle pressed a rather enthusiastic kiss to the back of my mother's hand, and I could only stand back and watch as my mother returned his praise in kind.

"Why, Beetle, you haven't changed a bit, either. Still a handsome devil, and just as charming to boot." My mother might have actually batted her eyelashes, but I'd been blinking mine too furiously to know for sure. It was never a pleasant sight to witness one's mother flirting with a man four years her senior. Or was it five? "I couldn't believe it when Raven told me that you were going to be helping out with the tea shop. She made such a wise choice in hiring you, and I told her as much."

Please tell me I'm hallucinating. Why is your mother looking at my BFF as if she were hit with that Cupid's arrow you were slinging around over Valentine's Day? You know, the one that had the entire town in an uproar. I can only take so much. And there it is—I think I've got another hairball caught in my throat.

I was too flabbergasted that my mother could lie with such ease about her reaction to Beetle's employment to answer Leo. I distinctly, and in great detail, recalled the ten to fifteen-minute lecture I received on hiring anyone to work in the tea shop. She'd been concerned—and rightly so—that Beetle might see something that would give away our family secret.

Your mother has always been the do as I say, not as I do *type.*

"Breathe," Heidi murmured, ordering me to sustain my life. She even gave me a slap on the back to get me started. "Let's just get your mother over to the diner before we need to bleach our eyes."

Having to solve the murder of a carnival worker that may have been committed by a warlock was bad enough, but to have my mother flirt with my new employee was a little bit too much. I could only handle so much of the amount of caffeine I'd consumed this morning—which wasn't nearly enough.

"Mom, we really should be heading over to the diner before it's too late to get a booth."

Chances are, we were already too late to grab a decent spot, and we'd be stuck at some table near the door, far away from all the good scuttlebutt happening in the clutch of booths with a sightline straight down the counter. Leo was right about my recent streak of bad luck.

"My beloved Regina, would you do me the honor of having dinner with me this evening?" Beetle asked, even giving my mother a small bow of enticement. His blue eyes sparkled with excitement in a way I haven't seen since he learned to use the cash register. "It would give us a chance to catch up and relive some of our glory days before you left."

I feel another hairball coming up.

"Mom." I really needed some air. Thankfully, Pearl had just walked past the display window, providing me with a legitimate reason to stop the direction of this conversation. "A customer is about to walk in, and we really should leave Beetle to his work."

"Beetle, I would love to have dinner with you," my mother crooned as if I hadn't said a word, causing Heidi to have to hide her amused smile behind her hand. I found absolutely nothing funny about this current quandary. "Let me spend some bonding time with the girls today, and then I'll meet you here at five o'clock so we can go out after you close."

I'm putting my paw down. I cannot—I repeat, cannot—put up with the both of you dating human males in a town this small. This is exactly how secrets get exposed, and now your mother has just gone and doubled the odds of our exposure. I'm now in need of a nap to rid me of all this anxiety.

"Raven and Heidi, are the two of you ready to begin our day of adventure?" Regina wiggled her fingers at a beaming Beetle before turning on the heel of her black ankle boot. It was like no one had died, and we weren't trying to solve a man's murder that quite possibly was linked to a very secret society we needed to keep under wraps. "I'd love to visit the fortune teller booth sometime today for the fun of it. Doesn't that sound like fun, girls?"

Pearl hadn't opened the glass door quite yet, but I'd been too focused on my mother to notice the reason why. I followed the older woman's gaze down the sidewalk, toward where the malt shop and Mindy's boutique were located, but there was no one in sight. Well, other than Leo, who'd managed quite ungracefully to leap back up into the display window.

"Beetle, I'll have my cell phone with me all day if there's an issue. I can be back here in under five minutes," I reassured him, patting the right pocket of my peacock skirt where I'd stored my phone. "Don't forget that Pearl's diffuser is on the top—"

Have you ever seen those videos of people setting cucumbers behind a cat to scare them? Or have you ever startled a cat by inadvertently making a quick movement or causing a loud sound?

Well, it was a wonder that Leo wasn't hanging from the ceiling by the tips of his scraggily claws.

Every strand of fur, even the tufts, was standing at attention as he arched his back in the most unnatural position. I'm pretty sure his right eye bulged out as much as his left, and his paws had levitated six inches off his pillow.

You see, the clown who had been at the scene of the murder last night had suddenly appeared smack dab in front of the display window. There had been no warning, no cued music like in the movies. No, there had been absolutely no foreshadowing of the clown's unexpected appearance.

Needless to say, Pearl made haste and was inside the tea shop before any of us could react. Heidi had let out a small yelp, and Beetle had laid a hand over his chest as if he were about ready to have a heart attack.

"I forgot to mention that I invited Buttons the Clown to breakfast," my mother announced, throwing a smirk Leo's way. "Aren't those happy pranksters just the best?"

Four

∽

"It's probably a good thing we left Leo back at the tea shop," Heidi murmured, hanging back as my mother and Buttons quickly grabbed a booth that was just now being vacated by Otis and Karen. The former sheriff and his wife seemed quite surprised to find that my mom was in town, and then there was Buttons in his full regalia. Regardless, they made small talk about the festival as if nothing was amiss before taking their leave. "Maybe I should have stayed behind. You know, talked business with Beetle. What time did I say was my first house showing?"

"You are *not* leaving me here alone with that trickster," I whispered back, pasting a smile on my face when my mother looked my way as she slid into the booth. "And you know darn well that I'm not talking about the clown, either."

My mother was up to her usual fare. We potentially had a murderous warlock in town who might very well have used his magic to take a human life, and my mother wanted to have breakfast with a clown, complete with makeup, in the only diner in town. I'd known for quite a while that my life had become rather...unconventional. Of course, this current masterpiece was all my mother's doing. Mixing warlocks with clowns was beyond my ability to guess at where she was coming from in the most remote fashion.

Speaking of the possible warlock in question, Rye was sitting at the counter next to Alfred and Eugene. The two older gentlemen were retired. They had plenty of free time, and they liked to play chess over at Monty's hardware store to pass the hours of the day. The three men seemed to be engaged in a debate over what wood made better fences in wet saltwater climates like ours. Could someone enjoy breakfast and have such a commonplace discussion over such a mundane subject after they'd murdered someone in cold blood? Only a psychopath would be capable of such behavior, in my judgment.

Heidi suddenly rushed by me, awkwardly sliding into our side of the booth. I'd been so caught up in listening to Rye's conversation that I hadn't noticed who'd taken what seat. It was then that I realized that she didn't want to be the one sitting across from the clown while she ate. My best friend had sacrificed me to the court jester who went by the moniker of Buttons.

"My name is Raven, and this is Heidi." I cautiously sat on the soft vinyl while keeping a close eye on my mother's guest, wondering if Heidi wasn't right about making an excuse to get out of Dodge. "I didn't know the two of you knew one another."

"Oh, we don't," Buttons fessed up with a really, really big smile full of gleaming white teeth. Who knew such a happy response could be so unsettling? "We ran into each other on the sidewalk, and your mother was kind enough to ask me to join you ladies for breakfast. I couldn't say no to such a beautiful woman. We carnies travel all over the country, and I have to say that the people here in Paramour Bay are just about the nicest bunch we've ever run into."

As expected, the diner was completely packed this morning. The vast majority of the patrons were year-round residents, with a few tourists sprinkled in amongst them, and a couple of added tables of carnival workers. It was easy to distinguish between the diners, due to the carnival's grey uniforms for their ride operators, food vendors, and game operators. The only one who stood out like a beacon was our friend Buttons, who had waved to his colleagues at one of the other tables. I'm sure his buddies would quiz him later about his good fortune.

As for Rye, my back was toward the counter. I couldn't see or hear what was now being said, so he definitely had me at a disadvantage. Did he find it strange that we were having breakfast with a clown in full makeup? If he were a warlock and the guilty party in Kevin Paul's murder, would Rye comprehend what we were doing here with the clown?

"Good morning," Paula said with a tentative smile on her face, standing a bit closer to me than Buttons. His red wig shook when his head swiveled her way. "What can I get you to drink? Coffee, tea, orange juice?"

My mother placed her coffee order as if sitting next to a clown in our little town's one true restaurant was the most natural thing in the world, not even bothering to reach for one of the menus that was stored behind the salt and pepper shakers. She'd become a huge fan of the pancakes, and it was doubtful that she'd try anything else anytime soon. Not once did she give away the fact that she had noticed Rye sitting at the counter.

"I'll have a tall glass of orange juice with a straw, please." Buttons pointed toward his painted lips while tipping his head and batting his false eyelashes. No, that wasn't creepy at all. "Oh, and a glass of water. Staying hydrated is very important."

Heidi and I quickly gave our drink orders, wanting this meal with our unexpected guest to be over as quickly as possible. If we could have requested some espressos instead of regular coffees, we might have been better equipped to deal with whatever my mother had gotten us into.

"So," my mother began the conversation, even giving Buttons a comforting pat on his gloved hand. "I told Buttons here how sorry we are about his friend. It's a terrible tragedy, just terrible. Have the police found any leads as to who would do such a horrible deed?"

I'd thought that maybe this was the direction my mother was going to take, but that didn't mean we couldn't have had the same outcome by just paying Buttons a visit at the carnival. Well, in all likelihood, Heidi and I would have sent my mother to talk to Buttons while we asked the other carnies questions that might lead to the answers we needed.

"I gave my statement to the sheriff last night." Buttons sniffled and looked a bit forlorn, but he didn't dare wipe his nose with a napkin. It did beg to question if he would remove the big red bulbous nose while he ate his breakfast. I can't imagine it was easy to wear such a thing while eating. "Poor Kevin. I hadn't known him long, but he seemed like a good guy. Always in a good mood and eager to get his work done. He joined the carnival over the winter when we were down south in Alabama, and he seemed rather excited that we were traveling north to start the new spring season. You were the one who found him, right?"

"Unfortunately, yes," I replied, reaching for the wrapped silverware next to the paper placemat to give myself something to do. It didn't escape me that Cora and Desmond Barnes were at their usual table. And as was typical, Cora was glaring my way. Well, more my mother's direction, but you know the old adage—only I was allowed to say bad things about my mother and get away with it. "I was taking the shortcut between the kissing booth and the dunk tank. I didn't realize until it was too late that Mr. Paul was lying on the ground at my feet."

"I don't understand why Kevin would have been on that side of the carnival when he'd been slated to work the tilt-a-whirl last night." Buttons had taken my lead and uncurled his napkin from the silverware. "It doesn't make any sense. He shouldn't have been there."

"Do you know why Mr. Paul was excited about traveling up this way?" my mother inquired, reaching over to the sugar holder to pull out two pink packets from among the other usual selection of sweeteners stored in a rectangular cut glass container. She tapped them against her hand. "Did he have family in the area that you know of?"

My mother continued to rhythmically tap the small pink envelopes as she repeated her battery of questions. The only reason I noticed the small dose of magic being utilized was the warmth in the palm of my hand. It was the same tingling sensation I developed when things started to go south around me, which meant someone else besides me was drawing on the energy surrounding us—my mother.

I'd already acknowledged that my mother had invited Buttons to breakfast to try and find some answers, but this was going a bit over the edge. If Rye really was a warlock, he'd be able to sense the undercurrent of energy just like me.

I had no choice.

I kicked my mother underneath the table...hard enough for her to notice.

47

Buttons practically came out of his seat, his pained expression coming through his face paint loud and clear.

"Ow!" Buttons practically yelled, reaching down underneath the table to rub his shin. He'd grabbed a lot of attention from the nearby diners. Heidi covered her pink lips the way she did when trying to hide a smile or laugh. As for my mother, she didn't look the least bit amused. "What was that for?"

"I'm so, so sorry," I apologized, reaching across the table but not touching his hand. The white gloves kind of freaked me out, but I had to give him credit. He looked at me with more curiosity than anger. "I was, you know, having trouble with a—Charley horse."

"It's those darn knee-high boots of yours, isn't it?" Heidi interjected with a shake of her head, entirely used to saving my hide in situations just like these. As I've mentioned before, I'm a horrible liar. Heidi? Not so much, but her heart was always in the right place. "They've been giving her problems lately. Were you trying to wedge your toes against the metal post underneath the table? You never did have any sense of aim."

Buttons appeared as if he wasn't too sure he should believe Heidi, but he eventually nodded his understanding.

"These clown shoes cause the arches of my feet to ache something fierce. They make it feel like I'm walking on bricks all day and night," Buttons shared, still showing a slight grimace of pain from where I'd kicked him in the shin. "I'm sorry, Ms. Marigold. What were you asking me?"

My mother had arched her perfectly waxed eyebrow my way in disappointment, but at least I'd gotten her to stop using magic in the diner. I snuck a quick glance over my shoulder to see that Rye was still in deep discussion with Albert and Eugene. What if I was wrong about everything?

"Kevin mentioned he had a friend in town here, and that

he'd grown up not too far from Paramour Bay," Buttons replied with a small shrug of his shoulders. "I told the sheriff all that last night, but I'm not sure it's enough information to help catch whoever killed Kevin."

Buttons looked as if he wanted to say more, but Paula must have been headed toward our table. The clown leaned back against the seat so that our waitress could set down our drinks. Three coffees were dispersed, along with one tall orange juice, a glass of water, and two straws.

"Why, thank you, miss," Buttons said in a rather squeaky tone before pulling a beautiful paper flower out of nowhere.

Paula's expression brightened as Buttons' kind gesture had apparently erased any doubt that he was a good-natured clown. I wasn't so sure about that, and I still had a few questions of my own to ask him. Unfortunately, a couple of the children in the diner took the flower as a signal that the show had begun, and that they could come over to the table and ask for animal balloons.

Buttons stood up and began his entertaining act, much to the delight of the patrons.

"Do not use *that* in here when a certain someone might notice," I warned, having leaned across the table to get my point across using subtle yet effective words.

"You want answers, this needs to be solved quickly, and I'm better at *that* than you."

I couldn't disagree with any of those points, especially the last one she'd emphasized. The discussion was about to be taken way off topic, but this was too good an opportunity to pass up.

"And why is that, Mother?" I asked, still being vague in case someone else was listening to us while Buttons was being kept busy by his audience. "For someone who gave up *that* such a long time ago, there seems to be no rusty spots, if you get my drift."

My mother leaned back against the cushioned vinyl of the booth and continued to stir her coffee as if I'd not pointed out the obvious. It was clear that I wasn't going to get any answers from her, but at least we had a moment to clear the air about who was making the tactical decisions right now.

"Why did you invite him to have breakfast with us, anyway?" I was still leaning forward and keeping my voice as low as possible. "We could have waited to talk to him later today without all this drama. I wanted to hear today's scuttle-butt, and you know how they all talk in here."

"Raven's right, because the booth behind me has done nothing but talk about the murder," Heidi chimed in, full of conspiracy, her whisper a little louder than ours. "Did you know that Kevin wasn't well-liked? Apparently, Buttons isn't being exactly truthful with us concerning his friend."

Heidi and I practically bumped heads when the laughing clown suddenly came back to our table with a big plop into the seat, causing my mother to lift a half an inch off her half of the vinyl cushion. It was a good thing she hadn't been holding the coffee cup to her lips.

"Aren't kids the best? They see the simple happiness of life, and it's my job to make sure it stays that way," Buttons said with a squeeze of his nose that actually beeped. He reached his white glove over the table and patted my hand that I had wrapped around my own cup. "I never got to really say how sorry I am that you were the one who found the body. I can only imagine how much of a shock it was to make such a discovery."

"We were just saying how the crime here in Paramour Bay is almost nonexistent," my mother exclaimed, casually reaching for another pink packet of sweetener. She stopped immediately once she caught sight of my pointed glare. "I know you mentioned that Kevin kept to himself, but do you think the killer could be someone you both knew? I mean, do you think the carnival is safe to be reopened?"

I shared a look with Heidi, who only managed to mouth the word *wow* at the fact that my mother never did have tact in these situations. She was like a bull in a china store.

"Of course, it's safe," I interjected, wondering if calling Mom in on this murder investigation had been the best decision. If Rye was truly a warlock, then indeed having my mother here was the best alternative. But I was seriously having my doubts that maybe I'd placed the call a teensy-weensy bit too early. "Mother, Liam and Detective Swanson would never have allowed the carnival to remain open if they thought for one second that it wasn't safe for the townsfolk."

"I have to agree with your daughter, ma'am." Buttons had dropped the squeaky tone for a brief moment, taking all of us by surprise at the deepness of his voice. He even made his eyes have a sad appearance despite the face paint. "There are some good folks who work with the carnival, and this is how we make our living. As for Kevin, isn't it true that not everyone gets along with everyone else? And the one person who would have had a grudge against Kevin is no longer with the carnival."

"What do you mean?" I asked, eager to mentally add someone to the suspect list. Right now, the list only includes Rye and Buttons himself. I had a sneaking suspicion there was more to the story, and I could only hope that it didn't include the coven. "Who would have a grudge against Mr. Paul?"

"Why, the same man who Kevin ended up getting fired in Florida—Elroy Simpson." Someone caught Button's attention, and his face lit up with joy. "Oh, look! Our breakfasts are here, and just in time. I'm starving!"

As Paula began unloading the meals from the tray in her hands, Heidi, my mom, and I all shared a look that spoke of promise. We were making progress, slow as it was, but we were a little bit closer to finding out who killed Kevin than we were five minutes ago.

Leave it to someone in my family to ruin the mojo.

"Wow, Ms. M.!" Heidi exclaimed, not even bothering to pick up her fork. Her nose was practically touching the window that faced the main thoroughfare in town. "I think I just spotted your doppelganger. That woman is the spitting image of you, only a bit older."

Neither my mother nor I needed to confirm who was walking across the street toward the diner, because there was only one woman who Mom was the spitting image of—Aunt Rowena.

"Mom, if Aunt Rowena is here…"

I let my words trail off and felt my heart thud against my chest when my mother only nodded her agreement, pursing her lips as she contemplated our next move. You see, there was only one reason why Aunt Rowena would be in the town of Paramour Bay.

Either Rye Dolgiram was the warlock we suspected him of being, Kevin Paul was murdered due to the brewing war between the factions of the coven, or worse—both.

Five

"I don't understand what just happened," Heidi murmured, looking over her shoulder in confusion as my mother and Aunt Rowena walked in the opposite direction. "Why aren't we going with them to find out why your great-aunt has shown up in town? She might have the very answers we're looking for."

"Two reasons, really. First, Aunt Rowena is used to dealing with a community full of witches, for which Mom is better equipped at handling her. Second, she kinda-sorta found out that you know our little secret when we had to go to Windsor to save that fairy. I'd rather not find out her feelings on the subject," I responded warily, resisting the urge to secretly follow them. I made an attempt to peer into the tea shop's display window in hopes that Leo would see we were now heading down Water Way. The first listing Heidi was going to look at was in ten minutes, but we could walk there in five. "Trust me, Mom will find out exactly what's going on and then call me with any news."

Well, at least that was the current plan. Aunt Rowena and my mother didn't get along very well, but that had more to do with Nan leaving the coven than anything else. Aunt Rowena had kept to herself up in Windsor, and my mother and I did the same in our respective abodes. Should it turn out that Rye was a part of the coven and acting on the council's orders to take out a designated target, then we had a bigger problem on our hands—not that there was any indication that Kevin Paul was a warlock or anything like that, regardless that his hometown was Windsor, as was stated on his driver's license.

I tried to remind myself that the sun was still shining and spring was in the air. There were even a few puffy clouds scattered above, gracefully moving along their way out over the bay. According to the weatherman, we weren't supposed to receive rain until sometime later in the week. There was a slight chill hanging in the early morning air that would dissipate come this afternoon when the sunshine shared its adequate warmth. The uneasiness that had settled over me had nothing to do with the nippy temperature and everything to do with the impending witch war.

"We'll go see this house first before we walk over to the carnival. We aren't going to let anything untoward get in the way of you moving here at the end of the month. I need you here with me." We also needed to keep our day on track. The way the morning was progressing, it was as though we were running out of time before we had even gotten started. At least Mom knew where to find us if she needed us, and she would definitely call me first thing in case of an emergency. "We might not actually need to talk to any of the carnival workers if Mom finds out that Rye was the one who killed Kevin Paul. In the meantime, I hope that Leo—"

Why is my paw burning like the fire of Hades? Raven, there is something definitely wrong with this fairy stain on my fur. You need to fix it.

Oh, this wasn't good at all. Leo had somehow missed the unexpected arrival of Aunt Rowena. No wonder he hadn't materialized sooner. Honestly, I'm not sure how he could have missed something so monumental happening in the street right outside the shop.

Did you just say that Rowena is here? As in here, here? In Paramour Bay? In our town, specifically? Well, I have to give you props—that's one way to get my mind off this darn fairy stain. I hadn't thought of that one before.

Leo suddenly appeared in front of us, which wasn't quite as dangerous, seeing as we were on one of the side streets. He looked a bit ruffled, and he was holding up his right paw with a scowl of monumental disgust.

The lipstick stain, left behind by a fairy named Strife, was practically glowing. It did have me worrying a bit that the perpetual fairy dust attached to Leo's fur would radiate in such a manner when my great-aunt was in town. I wasn't exactly sure of the portent displayed by this sign, but it couldn't be a good omen. It had never done so before, so it was more about connecting the dots that we had available to us.

Long story short, the fairy we helped cross into the afterlife with her charge had left behind a thank-you kiss on Leo's fur, but I did have to wonder if she hadn't given Leo a mystical way of sensing when the coven was nearby. Maybe it had been her way of thanking us.

After all, a member of the council was the reason Strife had been held against her will on this plane of existence to begin with. The last time we'd been up in Windsor, Aunt Rowena had still been part of the council, although only in name. Only those in the afterlife knew what had happened since then. For all we knew, the two factions could be in open warfare by now.

It did beg the question if Rye wasn't some sort of henchman or maybe a spy who did the dirty work of the council. Had there been an open contract issued by the council on Kevin Paul? If so, why? Had Rye fulfilled his duty to remove any threats to the coven? What was he doing in Paramour Bay to begin with? Did the council have him here to watch me, or maybe something worse? So many questions.

Henchman? Contract? Wait a second. You weren't making that stuff up about Rowena being in town, were you? Oh, I need to sit down. If there's blood to be spilled on behalf of the coven, then Rowena is definitely the witch who would be involved. We want no part of this, Raven. None. Zero. Zilch. We need to arm ourselves and prepare for battle.

"Mom is taking care of Aunt Rowena," I reluctantly admitted, feeling as if we were losing control of this situation. As for Leo, he'd already been sitting on his haunches with his head on a swivel. I truly believed that my mother was a force to be reckoned with, but Aunt Rowena was like the evil queen to my peasant life among the village masses. Leo wasn't helping with my desire to remain calm, especially if he couldn't even tell if he was standing or sitting. "Aunt Rowena showed up in town around fifteen minutes ago, and that tells me Kevin Paul's murder has something to do with the coven. It's no matter of coincidence."

The palm of my hand tended to overheat when I became anxious, and it was definitely dialed up to ten at the moment. What had I been thinking to allow my mother to go off alone with Aunt Rowena? Wasn't divide and conjure a thing?

That's divide and conquer, you simpleton. You were thinking that I came first, and you'd be right. Let's go barricade ourselves in the cottage, offer Ted up as a ritual sacrifice, and Heidi can dance around the fire while we drink wine and smoke catnip, whilst figuring out what spell in the grimoire can make Rowena disappear.

"Heidi, I hate to do this to you, but do you think you can look at this one listing without me?" A bit of anger began to surface that I wasn't going to be a part of my best friend's decision to find the perfect house. My palm was beginning to pop with static electricity. "Leo is right. Aunt Rowena wouldn't be here if she weren't a part of this whole mess, and I've had enough of being kept on edge and constantly wondering when she would pay us a visit. It's time she understands that I'm going to stick to Nan's decision to live a life outside of the coven and their self-serving collection of puritan rules."

This Leo? As in, me Leo? We seem to have gotten our signals crossed, Raven. I might have a memory issue, but right now I'm very much of sound mind and body. I never said that a confrontation with a council member—your great-aunt in particular, whose vast powers are far superior to ours—was the way to go in this scenario. What I said was that we should barricade ourselves in the cottage, offer Ted up as a sacrifice, cuddle with Heidi, and consume as much catnip and wine as we can in the short amount of time we have left on this earth.

"That is so not what you said, Leo." I inhaled deeply to help with my composure, setting my hands on my hips as I tried to figure out a way out of this without Liam and the entire town finding out that the supernatural world exists. "I don't understand how this fell onto my shoulders. What is so wrong with a peaceful life as a tea shop owner who wants to help her best friend make a monumental, life-altering thirty-year decision? That's how long mortgage loans are, right?"

Heidi let out a light laugh and grabbed my hands, waiting for me to look at her before she did one of her legendary lectures that talked me down off the edge of the cliff.

I think I'm already in freefall. I need a golden parachute.

"Isn't it possible that your Aunt Rowena sensed that your mother was in town and came to visit?"

"I'm not sure that's something our family does," I replied cautiously, not seeing where Heidi was going with this speech. Usually, her first sentence did the trick. My anxiety ratcheted up another notch. "I don't know the strength of Aunt Rowena's power, only that she's much stronger than my mother, Leo, and I put together."

She's not handing me a parachute, Raven. I thought you said Heidi was good at giving pep talks.

"Coincidences happen all the time," Heidi reassured me, though she really didn't ease either Leo's or my tension level. "Rowena being in town might have nothing to do with Kevin Paul's murder at all. I mean, what about good ol' Elroy Simpson? Buttons even said that the man had an axe to grind and a bad temper. Well, maybe that last part was my own invention. What if this is simply a case of revenge? Elroy lost his job because of Kevin, and the man wanted revenge."

I don't know who this Elroy character is, but I'm about to hit the ground according to that earlier analogy and end up resembling a rather flat pancake. I want a different comparison, Raven. I don't care for pancakes.

"How can you say it's just a coincidence that Aunt Rowena is here the day after the death of a man who was raised in Windsor, along with the possibility that Rye Dolgiram is a reneged warlock? Heidi, everything is pointing toward the coven and the war that's brewing between the factions. This is bad. I mean, really bad."

My cell phone vibrated in my skirt pocket, and I instantly had the device against my ear without even taking a second to look at the display. I'd made some pretty bad mistakes in the past, and I hadn't known it in this exact moment, but this one would end up taking the cake.

"Please tell me that Aunt Rowena isn't here because of the murder," I begged, looking up into the tree branches that hung over the sidewalk from an old oak tree in one of the front yards. I was a bit surprised to see a fuzzy squirrel staring down at us as if he were a squirrel ninja ready to do combat with Leo. "I can only take so much stress at this point."

The awkward silence that followed was my first sign that something was majorly wrong. You know that moment when your body goes cold, and your stomach thinks the bottom has fallen out from under you? Well, I didn't want to pull my phone away from my ear to look at the display for fear of seeing that my mother's name wouldn't be showing on the screen.

You just escalated our already precarious situation tenfold, didn't you?

"Raven?" Liam had said my name somewhat guardedly, not that I blamed him. How was I going to get myself out of the mess I'd just made? "Why would your aunt be in town due to Kevin Paul's murder? Did they know each other? What gives?"

Leave it to Leo to just now notice the squirrel keeping a cautious eye on us from the tree branch.

Is that a...squirrel! Run for your lives!

Leo had just been praising himself about staving off his short-term memory issue, but he'd spoken too soon. He'd also taken the meaning of the word *squirrel* to a whole new level, and his hefty backside began to wiggle back and forth as if nothing else in this world existed but the furry-tailed rat squatting on the branch above us.

Now that I think about it, it was just last night that I was congratulating myself on balancing my relationship with Liam and keeping such an explosive secret that could potentially ruin everything.

Best laid plans and all that, right?

Heidi was glancing down at her watch, inadvertently reminding me that she had somewhere to be in short order. Leo had taken off as fast as his body weight could take him upward, eight or more feet into the oak tree, and I was left having to come up with some excuse that had some sort of plausibility as to why Aunt Rowena might be interested in a carnival worker's murder.

"Liam, how are things going with the investigation?" I asked, hoping to defer his need for an answer as long as possible. I made the decision to walk with Heidi, seeing as I had no idea where Mom and Aunt Rowena might have gone, so it would be futile to start roaming the streets of Paramour Bay. And I definitely didn't want to run into Liam in person. He'd for sure recognize the obvious signs of me lying through my teeth. "Heidi and I are taking a stroll through the neighborhood to the first listing the realtor scheduled for her."

I fell into step beside Heidi, whose blue eyes were practically glued to the phone in my hand as if it were about to grow legs. Her expression of horror pretty much summed up what I was feeling.

"Raven, you didn't answer my question."

I'd only ever heard Liam speak like that when he was addressing someone he was questioning as a suspect of a crime, and it practically broke my heart. With that said, I'd worked hard to have a balance between my two personas, and I wasn't ready to lose either one of them. Had I been given time to confer with Heidi, she would have told me that I should square my shoulders and dive headfirst into the problem.

"Oh, you mean about Aunt Rowena? You met her a few

months back when we drove up there to get my mother's sugar glider, remember? She's a hoot, isn't she? Anyway, she's one of those people who has a fascination with those true crime stories," I said, not giving myself time to hesitate. There was too much on the line, and Leo was currently MIA, attempting to hunt a squirrel he would never catch. "I know you have a lot on your plate, and I was just hoping that Aunt Rowena didn't show up with a ton of amateur sleuth questions and get in your way."

We'd finally arrived in front of the house that was first up on the listings Heidi had been given by the local realtor. As a matter of fact, the lady in question was waiting for us on the front stoop with a big "I hope you buy this one" smile on her face. I wish I felt so optimistic regarding the next five minutes or so, but Liam had yet to really comment on my so-called excuse.

"Speaking of which, how is it going today?" A part of me was hoping Liam would make some big announcement that he'd apprehended the killer, and the weekend plans we'd had to sneak sweet moments in between his schedule could stay the course. That wasn't so much to ask, was it? "I was hoping to stop by the station this morning, but my plans for today got away from us."

I certainly wasn't lying about that last part.

"Jack just put an all-points bulletin out on a man by the name of Elroy Simpson. Seems he had a grudge against the victim and was seen in town by some of the carnies we spoke to last night," Liam said, though I could still detect traces of uncertainty regarding my excuse about Aunt Rowena. "If Simpson is the man we're looking for, he's probably long gone by now. Just in case, keep an eye on your surroundings. Simpson is around six feet tall, with shaggy brown hair, brown eyes, and has a tattoo of Thor's hammer on his forearm."

"Heidi and I will be careful," I promised him, guilt settling deep inside my soul now that I'd had to once again lie to him. "After we take a look at this house, we're probably going to head over to the carnival. Will we see you there?"

"Yes, Jack and I are heading over that way now to do some follow-up questioning. How about we meet at eleven-thirty for an early lunch?" Liam sounded a little distracted, but he hung on the line until I gave the answer that Heidi and I would love to meet them at the food concession area. "Raven, you didn't tell me that your mother was in town, too."

Heidi had already made it down the narrow walkway to greet the realtor. They stood talking while I finished up my phone call, but it certainly wasn't ending the way I'd hoped.

"Um, Mom arrived first thing this morning, right before Aunt Rowena popped in," I tentatively answered, not wanting to know how he'd confirmed such a visit. A headache was starting to set up residence in my temples, and it wasn't one that any amount of aspirin could eradicate. Maybe he'd simply caught sight of Mom at the carnival. After all, I was an optimist. "Are you already at the carnival?"

"No, I'm still at the station." Liam must have put his hand over the receiver of his cell phone, because his words were muffled as he spoke to someone else. I was really, really hoping that he was carrying on a side conversation with Eileen, his dispatcher, but I couldn't be so lucky. "Send them in. Raven, I've got to go. It appears that your mother and aunt are here to see me. Remember, keep your eyes open."

Liam disconnected the line, leaving me standing on the sidewalk with my cell phone in hand and no one on the other end but doubt. My stress level was now through the roof. Why would my mother ever, under any circumstances, take Aunt Rowena to see the man I was currently dating? Was she completely and utterly insane?

To make matters worse, Leo came running down the sidewalk as fast as his short little legs could carry him, and looking a little worse for wear—and that was saying a lot.

Can squirrels give cats rabies? I'm asking for a friend, but it's really urgent.

"Leo, I can't handle your conspiracy squirrel questions right now. We have a bigger problem," I explained to him, leaning down so it didn't look odd that I was talking to my cat. Thankfully, Heidi and the realtor had already headed inside the house. "You need to go to the police station to find out why Mom and Aunt Rowena sought Liam out. Mom's conversation with Aunt Rowena must have gone really sideways, and I can't get there in time to stop them from doing whatever it is they think they're doing. I trust you, Leo. The future of our lives here in Paramour Bay now rests on your shoulders. Make it happen."

Six

That squirrel thought I had broad shoulders, too. Jumped out of that tree like he was the one with a parachute, and I'm the one who ended up with the battle scars. Raven, am I foaming at the mouth yet?

"Did Rowena really block Leo from entering the police station?" Heidi asked as we walked through the numerous tourists and residents who were enjoying the entertainment and beautiful weather. She sidestepped two excited children as they raced toward the twirling teacups. "You're dating Liam. How does your aunt and mom believe we're not going to find out what they were doing this morning?"

Now that I think about it, that glyph of a warding spell was pretty strong. There's no doubt that Rowena is up to something because she would have had to prepare that spell in advance. I suppose that I could always take her out with rabies.

"That's exactly what frightens me, Heidi." The tingling in my palm hadn't subsided. It was a constant static that was beyond annoying, and I wanted it to stop. I wanted everything to go back to the way it was before Leo caught Rye using magic on my gate to dispel my ward, and way before Kevin Paul's murder. "What if Aunt Rowena did something to Liam? You know, erased his thoughts or his feelings toward me. Mom should have called me by now."

It would also explain why I didn't feel Rowena's presence earlier when she first arrived in town. She must have carried the glyph on a talisman. On a side note, squirrels aren't known for hunting wounded cats, right?

I couldn't stop rubbing my right palm with my other thumb in an attempt to lessen the distracting sensations. It felt like my hand had fallen asleep—pins and needles. If I thought for one second that Liam wouldn't find it odd that I needed to cancel our early lunch, I'd do it in a heartbeat. As it stood currently, the only chance of finding out why Aunt Rowena and my mother had sought out Liam was to ask him myself.

I startled when Leo's four paws all lifted off the ground at the same time, but thankfully, he'd had enough wherewithal not to disappear into thin air amongst the crowded people.

"A flower for the pretty lady?" Buttons bellowed with a smile, bringing us up short when he jumped in front of our path toward the picnic tables. In the grip of his white glove was a purple carnation. "How about two?"

Leo hissed at Buttons from behind the corner of the funnel cake stand. Buttons didn't seem too fazed at the sight of a pet cat walking with his owner around a carnival. Well, maybe he had given a second glance, but he was too busy waiting for us to take the purple and pink carnations out of those freaky white gloves that still didn't have a smudge of dirt on them.

I hate clowns. Not as bad as squirrels, but they're right up there on my list with spiders and fairies.

"Thank you, Buttons," I said, following suit after Heidi had already expressed her appreciation. I glanced over his shoulder toward the pizza stand, but I couldn't find Liam anywhere in the crowd. Maybe I could get some questions answered, though. "How is today going for everyone? I can imagine that it's been pretty rough on everyone to keep up the momentum for the children and their parents after last night's tragedy."

Buttons cautiously looked around before taking a step closer. It didn't escape my notice that Heidi took a small step to the side as Leo cautiously approached while keeping her between them.

I'm not taking any chances. Besides, I've got to save up my energy in case I have another round with Skippy the Squirrel. I can't let bygones be bygones after what he did to me this morning. Death before dishonor.

"Word has it that Elroy Simpson was seen in town yesterday," Buttons whispered, holding up one of his pristine white gloves near his painted face as if we were conspiring with one another. "Get this. Kevin didn't only take Elroy's job, but he also moved in on the man's girlfriend, too. Turns out that Clara spent all night crying in Kevin's camper over what happened to him. Poor thing. Olive took the day off to stay with her in the camper, although George wasn't too happy about being shorthanded."

"George?" It was pretty easy to follow Button's story. Clara had been Kevin's girlfriend, and Olive was the best friend. It sounded as though George was one of the bosses, but it was always best to clarify who was who in this situation. "I take it George makes the schedule for the staff?"

The day might just be looking up if there were more suspects to put on the list. Maybe I'd overreacted about Aunt Rowena being in town. It could have simply been as Heidi had suggested—Aunt Rowena sensed my mother's presence and came to visit. Most likely, Aunt Rowena was recruiting for the faction she was currently leading against the other council members of the coven. That left Rye to be the handyman he claimed to be, and I'd only allowed my imagination to run wild when it came to my gate.

"George Mertes is the owner and operator of this small outfit. He had to use a couple of local volunteers to cover for the others." Buttons lowered his hand and wiggled those gloved fingers at a couple of passing children and their moms. He once again looked all around us, almost as if George was going to pop out from behind the carousel. "Clara and Olive have been with the carnival for years, like me. We're already short-staffed, and George has a lot on his plate now that one of his employees was killed during open hours. He'll be lucky if his insurance isn't revoked. We even had to shut down one of the less frequented rides so that we had enough workers to man the other attractions and the game booths. On top of that, I heard through the grapevine that the state detective has been all over George, looking for answers as to why Kevin wasn't where he was supposed to be when he was killed."

Did that mean Jack and Liam suspected George Mertes of killing Kevin Paul?

Buttons had inadvertently given me information that could be very useful, and I couldn't wait to follow up on it. All Heidi and I had to do now was meet Liam and Jack for an early lunch, find out why Aunt Rowena and Mom felt the need to speak to Liam, and then Heidi and I would be able to walk over to the small campers in the far field to have a conversation with Clara and Olive.

Uh, Raven? There might be a small squirrel-sized wrench in your plan. I mean monkey wrench. Sorry, I've got squirrels on my mind.

"Look out for your pigtails, young lady! Oink, oink!" Buttons exclaimed, turning his attention to an adorable blonde child whose bottom lip began to poke out in fear. She even tried to hide behind her mother's leg, but Buttons had already pulled out a yellow balloon to distract her. "What's your favorite animal? Come on, you can tell me. I can make any animal you want, little one!"

"A squirrel!" the little girl squealed in delight.

Go figure. Those squirrels are out to get me, Raven, but from the sight before us...we might be dead soon anyway. I hope Skippy will feel cheated.

Heidi was already pulling me away from Buttons, tugging on my wrist to let me know Leo hadn't been exaggerating. Not that she knew that Leo had said anything at all about our impending deaths, but I'd put two and two together and came up with—four. Specifically, Aunt Rowena, my mother, Liam... and Rye. All four of them were literally standing fifteen feet from us looking like they were having anything but a merry ole time.

I hope she bestows a quick death upon us. At least I'll have escaped death by squirrel rabies. That's something, right?

"Whatever your great-aunt has done, don't overreact," Heidi muttered, trying to instill a bit of composure in me. Well, there was nothing she could do to stop my anxiety level from reaching the highest level at the sight before us. "You're the better witch, Raven. There's nothing you can't handle."

You might want to remind Heidi about the last few mishaps you had with those fairly easy spells. We wouldn't want her to die with the false hope of you becoming her heroine.

"Aunt Rowena," I called out, having no choice but to put on a show in front of Liam. I forced a smile that probably didn't quite meet my eyes, but it was better than nothing.

"Mom said you might be stopping into town to visit with us. I hope you haven't been keeping Liam too distracted looking after you, considering he's busy with the investigation."

"Raven, dear," Aunt Rowena called out, spreading her arms open for me to step into her embrace. "It's so good to see you. I'm so glad we reconnected, letting bygones be bygones and all that. When I heard about the murder of that poor man, I just had to make the drive down here."

It's a trap, Raven. Don't fall for it. Even snakes can smile.

It wasn't like I had a choice but to close the distance between us and greet her as if she'd told the truth. Her perfume was a bit strong, but that wasn't what had the air catching in my throat. It was the abject look of horror on my mother's face.

It appears I'm not the only one who's had a bad day. I wonder if your mother had a run-in with Skippy. That would certainly explain it. He's actually quite vicious.

"It's good to see you, Aunt Rowena. How is everything up in Windsor?"

It's never good to see her, Raven.

"Good, good, but I just couldn't believe it when we got word that Mr. Paul had been so brutally murdered in the street." Aunt Rowena finally allowed me to pull away and feigned that she couldn't hear a word Leo said. "The newspaper said that Mr. Paul was from our area, but I didn't know him personally. The next-door neighbor told me early this morning, before my little road trip, that Mr. Paul's family moved away a few years ago after he left the area. I thought your nice sheriff might want to know that."

That was news to me, especially considering that the address listed on Mr. Paul's license stated that his permanent address was still located in Windsor.

Raven, I'm getting the sense from your mother that it doesn't matter what address was listed on Mr. Paul's driver's license. Is it just me, or does she look a little pale?

"Hi," Liam finally said, giving me a wink of reassurance. I allowed myself a small reprieve and closed the distance between us, allowing his warm embrace to reassure me that no damage had occurred as a result of my great-aunt. "Heidi, did you like the house?"

You're right. The good ol' sheriff isn't looking at you the way your mother appears to be looking at Rye. This can only mean one thing. It's a good thing we haven't had lunch yet.

"It was really cute," Heidi offered up with a tentative smile, her gaze landing upon everyone for brief seconds at a time in an attempt to read their expressions. "We have two more to look at —one this afternoon and one tomorrow morning. I don't want to rush into such an important commitment without seeing every option available."

If we live that long. Rowena, fess up. What are you doing here?

Liam's warm hand continued to stay on my lower back as we all sort of fell silent, my mother and Rye still not joining in on the casual banter. Aunt Rowena didn't give any indication that Leo was talking to her, which was good considering our current circumstances.

I'm going to go out on a limb here. Not to where that ninja squirrel hangs out, but more figuratively. Are you ready?

I wasn't ready for anything Leo might have to say in this situation, so I asked the obvious question to hopefully forestall whatever horrible plan he'd come up with.

"Are we all having lunch together?" I asked, secretly hoping that everyone would say no and go their separate ways. Well, except for Liam. I'd still like to know what was said in his office. "Buttons was just telling us how good the pizza is here."

Rye, we know you committed the murder. Admit it. Go ahead. Admit that you killed the man, that you can hear every word I'm saying, and that you're a warlock. Do it now!

Had I not been looking directly at Rye to see his reaction to Leo's rusty interrogation skills, I would have missed the slight narrowing of the corners of his eyes.

You can thank me later. In premium catnip. Or a drawn and quartered squirrel named Skippy. Your choice.

"Actually, I have to meet Jack over by the campers. He wants to speak with the owner of the carnival regarding the firing of Mr. Simpson prior to the start of the spring season." Liam squeezed my hand before he stepped away, nodding toward Aunt Rowena. "Ma'am, it's always a pleasure. Please visit us again soon. I hope my suggestions for alarm companies pan out for you, and the company can get someone out to your residence first thing Monday morning."

Raven, I think my short-term memory kicked in. Alarm companies for a coven of witches? Now isn't that a novel concept?

"Sheriff Drake, my niece lucked out with a man like you," Aunt Rowena said in approval that was exclusively reserved for my mother. Who, by the way, still looked as if the squirrel that had landed on Leo's back had done the same to her hairdo. "I'm sure we'll be seeing each other real soon."

I'm pretty sure Rowena just threw down the gauntlet.

It sounded more like a promise, and I was going to make sure that it was one Aunt Rowena would regret.

Liam began to walk in the direction I'd wanted to take earlier, but it was clear I had some family business to attend to that my mother had let spiral out of control.

It's a good thing your mother can't read your thoughts. I'm sure she'd take offense to your lack of confidence in her abilities.

"Someone please tell me what is going on," I demanded,

finally taking control of the situation. I abruptly turned to face all three of my targets, grateful that Heidi came to stand by my side, as she might need my protection from Rowena if things went south. Heidi knew full well that Aunt Rowena was a part of the council of a very powerful coven, but Heidi didn't let that make a dent in her loyalty to me. That was a true best friend. "Now."

Very assertive. Nicely done. I wonder if that tactic would work on Skippy.

"Do they sell wine here?" my mother asked, exhaustion lacing her tone. She even rubbed her right temple as if she'd developed a headache. Well, at least I wasn't the only one. After all, misery did love company. "Aunt Rowena, you can go. Rye and I will explain everything to Raven. Your secret will remain safe with us, with the caveat that you'll leave us out of this war you're leading one half of the coven against the other on the end of your broomstick."

It's beginning to look like a free-for-all with all these personal slights I'm hearing. While we're airing our dirty laundry—I don't believe Rowena has all her broomsticks lined up in a row, if you get my drift.

"Leo, you're one tail swipe away from becoming a toad."

"Everyone, just stop the commentary."

Rye stepped forward, front and center.

Leo, Heidi, and I all took a step back in immediate reaction. I thought it was pretty smart on our part, though Rye arched one of his black eyebrows our way in chagrin.

"Mom, you can go back home," Rye advised softly, resting his gaze specifically on me. I was pretty sure that Heidi, Leo, and I all looked like we'd just heard he'd been hatched by an alien from Mars. "I'll touch base after Liam finds out who killed Kevin Paul. I appreciate you coming here, but I did have everything well in hand."

Your suggestion about him being an alien isn't that far off, you know.

Leo completely vanished when Aunt Rowena lifted her hand in response to his insult. A quick look around assured me that no one had seen his disappearing act, but we couldn't afford to take chances like that again. It was time to bring this so-called family visit to an end.

"Mom? As in, you're Rye's mother?" I asked, needing some type of confirmation that I hadn't taken up Leo's habit of hallucinating things. Then again, it seemed that Leo hadn't hallucinated anything at all. "This is what is going to happen. We're all going to sit down at that picnic table over there, each one of you is going to start from the beginning, and Heidi is going to go find us some of that wine Mother mentioned."

Is it safe to come back now?

Seven

You should have stipulated to Regina that she needed to bring catnip to this shindig, as much as I love her company. I find it hard to deal with three Marigold women at the same time without a buffer of some sort. It's next to impossible, and Rosemary never uttered a word about this type of reunion when she talked me into this gig.

I rubbed my temple, wishing my headache would dissipate as fast as Aunt Rowena's raised hand had precipitated Leo's earlier vanishing act. We were all currently sitting at one of the picnic tables off to the side of the funnel cake stand, away from all the normal, everyday families spending their Saturday afternoon enjoying the local entertainment in the fresh spring air. The live band had started playing down at the end of the carnival's thoroughfare, drawing the crowds in that direction. The rhythm of the folk music mixed with the beeps, dings, and rings of the rides farther down from the food vendor area.

The fresh spring atmosphere isn't so relaxing when I'm surrounded by three generations of Marigold witches. Wait, I already mentioned that, didn't I? That must be my short-term memory loss kicking in again. Stress does that to me, you know.

I was having a very hard time swallowing the story that Aunt Rowena and Rye had concocted out of thin air, but I couldn't find any glaring holes in their versions of the past events. With that said, it didn't take away the awesome wave of shock that had enveloped us once we discovered Rye considered Aunt Rowena a maternal figure.

That's kinda like saying I view Skippy as my fraternal twin. If that doesn't tell you the man is off his flipping rocker, I don't know what does. Time to break out the big guns!

"Look, dearest, I've been away from Windsor longer than I'd intended to be today. I have plans that need attending to posthaste." Aunt Rowena sat poised on the end row opposite me on the picnic table with her hands resting on top of the black purse that was currently sitting in her lap. She held an air of usurped royalty, and I could understand why someone—particularly Leo—would want to knock her right off that pedestal. Her position was stolen from its rightful owner, my grandmother, whom Aunt Rowena had driven from the throne of the witches' coven with lurid tales of willful disobedience. "Rye can finish filling you in on our situation. In the meantime, I left my familiar in a rather precarious situation up in Windsor."

I remember Gus. Never liked the chap, but it's hard not to have sympathy for a fellow familiar having to deal with the bizarre circumstance of keeping the queen bee of Windsor.

"No one is going anywhere just yet," I said adamantly, steadfast in my desire to finish this conversation with all parties involved present and accounted for. I picked up the coffee that Heidi had brought back, who had been unable to find a vendor serving wine or beer at eleven-thirty in the morning. Unfortunately, I wasn't so sure this small amount of my favorite beverage contained enough caffeine to enable me to get through the next five minutes. "Let me make sure I understand the manure you're selling. You found Rye as a wandering orphan in the city of Hartford when he was fourteen years old, and simply decided to bring him home with you? Just like that? No one took notice?"

Who knew that Rowena had an itsy-bitsy strand of maternal instinct buried deep underneath that overwhelming vanity? More like the Pied Piper of Hartford. Did some poor family fail to pay the ransom?

"Leo," I warned, shooting him a sideways glance. He was curled up in Heidi's lap near the opposite end of the table, as far away from Aunt Rowena as he could get. Regrettably, the distance wasn't far enough to protect him should Aunt Rowena truly dispense with a bit of magic from the tips of her fingers. "Stop instigating, or you'll be sorry."

You take the fun out of everything. Where's my pipe?

"Raven, I lost my parents at a young age, and the foster home the state put me in wasn't the most pleasant place to live." Rye was wearing his usual patterned flannel shirt, the kind he usually wore when working on the job. He gripped his coffee in his right hand while leaning both arms against the table. He seemed more resigned to explaining his story than anything else, but I steeled myself from feeling any empathy since this was most probably all a lie. He'd lied to me before. "I took to the streets, not knowing about..."

Rye had finally begun to open up about his accidental discovery of his abilities, but two teenage girls chose that moment to walk past while chitchatting about an upcoming concert they both wanted to go to later that evening. Rye took a drink of his coffee while he waited for the coast to clear of bystanders. During that brief lull, I reflected on what had crossed my mind in regard to Rye lying. Was I really one to judge another for doing exactly the same thing I was doing to someone else? Wasn't I playing the same game with Liam?

Rye gave a casual glance over his shoulder to make sure the coast was clear and that the funnel cake vendor wasn't listening in before finishing his story. It didn't escape my notice that his physical attributes did look similar to the Marigold lineage. He had the same black hair, green eyes, and high cheekbones. If that were in fact true, then why would they pretend he was an orphan and not his birth mother? Granted, Aunt Rowena was in her seventies now, but stranger things had happened. Now that I think about it, Rye had missed out on the hips, but maybe that was only an attribute on the female side. Were Aunt Rowena and Rye hiding something else? Could Rye truly be a Marigold and not some random gypsy with a magical family legacy?

"I found myself in what you might call a tricky situation behind the building of a restaurant. One thing led to another, and my innate sense defended itself. To say I was surprised is an understatement. You should have seen the shock on my assailant's face. Mom—Rowena—witnessed the entire interaction and immediately recognized my fear of the unknown and the true nature of my abilities. I'm not afraid to admit that I was downright panicked. Had it not been for her taking charge of the situation, I'm not sure I wouldn't have actually hurt someone sooner or later." Rye was no longer the little boy who Aunt Rowena found out back of a restaurant, probably near some dumpster, but he'd obviously been raised to have manners and some sort of moral guideline. His slight nod her way was a private acknowledgment of the care, love, and guidance she'd apparently given him over the years. It was difficult to begrudge anyone such a sacrifice, and she'd obviously raised a gentleman in spite of his rough origins. "Bottom line? Rowena took me in when I had no place else to go, and she raised me like her own son."

I'm just pointing out that I'm behaving myself and missing a lot of opportunities where I could have inserted my witty replies. Alas, I will remain silent and keep on alert for Skippy and his tribe of bandits.

"Why are you in Paramour Bay, Rye? Were you sent here originally to keep an eye on my grandmother and then me after she'd passed? Or are you here to somehow recruit me into this war Aunt Rowena has chosen to stir up among the members of the coven?" I shot Leo a look when it was clear he couldn't contain himself. Heidi lifted the corner of her lip in sympathy when I continued my quest to find some answers. "First off, I don't like being spied on. Second, Mom and I already made it very clear that we want no part of the coven, its council, or the war between whatever factions have managed to survive the carnage so far."

"His business is too established to be here only for you," my mother chimed in with what sounded like defeat, but I knew her better than that. She was busy tapping her red fingernail on the wooden surface of the table when she directed her next statement toward Aunt Rowena. "I think I figured it out. You sent him here some time ago when you recognized what would be coming down the road, to be away from Windsor before the first stone was thrown, didn't you? You didn't want him in harm's way, so you sent him to the one place where you knew he could find help if it was ever needed."

Aunt Rowena cleared her throat, visibly uncomfortable and not wanting anything to do with the sentimentality of this conversation. Either that or she didn't want to admit that she actually had a heart that pumped warm red blood. *Had* she sent Rye away to protect him? It was more than evident she'd wanted to be long gone before she was forced to give a viable explanation. Something had clearly happened that she'd felt the urgent need to ensure Rye's safety today of all days. The pieces of the family puzzle were beginning to fall into place, and I attempted to make another guess at her motives.

"Paramour Bay was good enough for your sister, so it had to be good enough for the young man you considered a son," I speculated, hitting close to home when I saw Aunt Rowena's gaze land on Rye with affection. I then switched my attention toward the man in question. "You made the mistake of *fixing* my gate, and Leo caught you in the act."

"In my defense, I didn't know your grandmother had a ward on the wrought iron fence. Otherwise, I would have left well enough alone. It was just as big a surprise to me as it was to you. I have stronger natural abilities than sometimes I can control, and one small link in your layered protection spell was dispelled before I could comprehend the damage I'd done to your grandmother's security system."

Great. Just great. As if one Marigold with a penchant for goofing up powerful magical spells wasn't enough, we now have Schleprock the Warlock on the loose in Paramour Bay. It's a wonder the town has survived as long as it has.

"Just so you know, I came back that night and negated the damage I'd done. You'll certainly know if someone or something crosses into your yard without your permission."

I wasn't so sure about that, because the gate still didn't make a sound when being opened. Then again, the only ones to cross the threshold of the property line had been Liam, Heidi, and my mother—all on my approved guest list.

"Now that we've settled everything, it's time I bid you

farewell and return to Windsor," Aunt Rowena stated matter-of-factly and with what sounded like a bit of relief before attempting to stand when my mother all but yanked our aunt and her purse back down with a plop. She gave an audible sigh of irritation. "What more would you like to know, dearest niece? I've all but admitted that my sister did the right thing by leaving the coven. The council wants to rewind our members back into the Stone Age. The members of the coven had a problem with not knowing exactly who Rye's birth parents were, and they all but threatened to throw him out if we didn't give permission to call upon his ancestors. Of course, I said I wouldn't have such nonsense."

That little zing I got when something wasn't right once again made itself known. Aunt Rowena was still hiding something, but I doubted any of us would get her to spill it anytime soon.

"I've been in Paramour Bay since the age of eighteen years old, but Mom explicitly forbade me to tell Rosemary about our situation unless the worst happened," Rye explained with a small shrug of concession. "She's never steered me wrong. So, I did the only thing I could and established a life here in anonymity. We meet at a little mom and pop café in between Windsor and Paramour Bay once a week."

"I will also have you know that I attempted to call on your grandmother once, but that stubborn wax henchman of hers refused to let me speak to her," Aunt Rowena confessed, clearly still upset by the rebuke after all these years. She tightened her grip on her purse as she finished her story. "It was pointless to continue reaching out to Rosemary when I was well aware she wanted nothing to do with me or the coven. I guess I don't blame her, given how things went down the day she left. I certainly said my fair share of hurtful words, but I don't regret sending Rye here to live. He was able to make a life for himself, while at the same time keeping an eye on my sister...and now my niece. Whatever you may think of me, my dearest Raven, I'm not the monster that I've been portrayed as being."

Arguable, but some of that story rings true. Didn't Ted say that Rowena called, going on and on about something to do with bread? And Mazie, the ghost we helped to find her familiar...she mentioned that Rosemary was fixated on the bread in the after-life. She must have figured out who Rye was the moment she crossed into the afterlife and tried to warn us that we had a spy in our midst.

"Dolgiram." Heidi cocked her head to the side, her blonde curls following. Leo couldn't control his inherent instincts and took a playful swipe, missing by an inch due to the shortness of his legs. "It doesn't quite spell Marigold backward, but I'd say it's darn close. You're a sly one, Mr. Rye Dolgiram, I'll give you that."

How had I missed something so blatantly evident? Leo and I were known as the amateur sleuths of the supernatural realm, but we had obviously come up lacking when it came to recognizing the obvious clues right there in front of us.

Heidi is part of our sleuthing package, you know. Technically, she figured it out. A little late, but it still counts.

"Why tell us all this now?" my mother asked, looking a bit more composed than earlier. Had she found something to spike her coffee? "You realize you brought attention to yourself the moment you marched into Liam's office and gave Rye an alibi for Kevin Paul's murder."

"You did what?" I asked, not sure I'd heard Mom correctly.

"I cleared my son's name," Aunt Rowena defended herself, lifting her chin an inch higher to prove her point. "Rye, did I not pay you a visit yesterday around five o'clock? Were we not together for an hour discussing our current predicament?"

Convenient, if you ask me. About as convenient as it was for Skippy to deflect my earlier attack on him with an offensive attack of his own.

"Yes, we were together during the time Kevin Paul was murdered," Rye answered, zeroing in on me. "The minute I heard my brochure was found in the man's hands, I realized that the police would focus their investigation on me. The last thing I need is the attention of law enforcement, so I did what any normal human being would do under the circumstances—I made sure Liam knew I had an alibi. A simple phone call would have sufficed, but Mom thought it was time to come clean with you and Regina. Too many things were getting out of hand, and we needed to control the situation before it caused unwanted conflicts."

I've got to admit it, Raven—they're good. It makes you almost believe them, doesn't it?

"So, let me get this straight," I said, trying to wrap my head around this overload of supplemental information. Liam had not acted as if I'd kept a secret from him, nor did he seem as if he was upset that I had a so-called cousin in town that I hadn't told him about. "You went into the sheriff's office, told the man I'm dating that you're my cousin, and somehow made it so that he wasn't upset I hadn't been completely honest about our alleged family connection."

"Not quite," my mother fessed up before taking a rather long sip of her coffee. If I hadn't known any better, I would have assumed that she *had*, in fact, spiked it with something. "It all went down like this—Rowena was in need of a handyman, you gave her Rye's name based on his work at your house, and then she decided to meet with him in person to go over her plans of including a remodel of her basement. That is how everything went down this morning, and now you are in the clear of having to explain our complicated family dynamics to the man you're currently dating. Aunt Rowena tied that red ribbon perfectly."

They're even better than I realized, and now I feel like we need to up our game. Raven, what are your thoughts about bringing an enemy spy on board this sleuthing gig we've got going on? He can do all the grunt work, Heidi can be the brains, and I can sit back on my cushion—I mean, throne— and direct them while you and Beetle bring me copious amounts of catnip.

My general thoughts weren't anywhere close to what Leo was suggesting. At the end of this long day, I would still be lying to the man I was falling in love with each and every day that passed. I was as bad as Aunt Rowena and Rye.

I don't know if I'd go that far...

"I'm not joining any detective team you've dreamed up," Rye replied wryly with a shake of his head while giving Leo a sideways look. "I still want what I've wanted all along—to live here in peace without the threat of being exposed or the need for violence. Mom knows that she can call on me if things go south up in Windsor, but other than that, I'm keeping my head down and continuing living the life that's been laid out before me."

All of this explained so much in the overall scheme of things, but there were still a few unanswered questions. I figured Heidi and I had about two more hours before we needed to show up at the next listing, which was around three o'clock this afternoon. I also needed to stop in at the tea shop to make sure Beetle was handling everything on that end. The shop had been at the back of my mind this entire time, and now another worry had been added to my plate about lying to Liam.

I'm pretty sure that's the least of our worries, but there's a bright spot in this somewhat tarnished family drama. Look at it like this—we no longer need to get involved with the factions of the coven. Breadman here can do all the legwork in helping Rowena when the time comes, and we can keep things status quo on our end.

"What about Kevin Paul? Did you know him or his family?" I asked Aunt Rowena specifically, seeing as she was the one who'd mentioned a neighbor knowing the Paul family. "Was he in any way associated with the coven? It's not like we can let the man's murder go unsolved if witchcraft was involved."

Are you purposefully trying to make our lives more difficult? We've cleared Breadman of the evil act, and now the good ol' sheriff can do his small part by apprehending the law-offending party. Win-win.

"Kevin Paul has nothing to do with the coven," Aunt Rowena replied, appearing ready to stand up and leave now that she felt she'd rectified the situation. She hadn't, but that battle was for another day. "The Paul family lived in another neighborhood, a very long time ago, and far away from the coven. He wasn't a warlock that I know of, and him being from Windsor is nothing more than a coincidence. As for what I told your Liam, I simply made all that stuff up about my neighbor. It seemed like a good idea at the time. Now, I've got to head back. Any further questions you might have can be directed toward Rye. I keep nothing from him, and he's aware of the truth."

True to her word, Aunt Rowena stood from the picnic table in her black pantsuit that didn't dare have a speck of lint on the fabric and proceeded to lay the straps of her purse over her shoulder. Rye had instinctively followed suit, swinging his legs over the bench seat to stand and give her a kiss on the cheek.

That was actually slightly nauseating. Rowena, I'd say it's been a pleasure, but we both know that's not the case. Feel free to stay up north longer this time, if that's something you can manage without our help.

"Call me when you arrive home," Rye instructed warmly, his feelings for Aunt Rowena evident. I caught the roll of my mother's eyes, apparently agreeing with Leo, but at least she'd kept her opinion to herself. "Drive safe."

"Will do, darling."

Aunt Rowena didn't even bother to address the rest of us as she began walking away toward the exit of the carnival, mindful of any divots in the grass.

I wonder if Skippy is open to bribes. I'd pay to see a squirrel run up her—

"Leo," I said, once more in warning. I was well aware of my relationship with my mother. I was allowed to be irritated by her annoying habits, but I couldn't stand it when others pointed out her flaws. My sense of loyalty was a bit lopsided, but it was still there all the same. I'm sure the same went for Rye regarding Aunt Rowena. "Have some respect."

"I can honestly say that wasn't how I thought our day would pan out," my mother said, finishing off what was left of her coffee. She was definitely more relaxed than when we'd first sat down. She cast a curious glance Rye's way, who still hadn't rejoined us at the table. "I guess we should welcome you to the family."

I'm not so sure that's good news, Regina. I mean, out of all the families he could have joined...

"I, for one, am very proud to be Marigold," I declared with

pride. We might have our fair share of family drama, and I might only know of my mother's lineage, but I wouldn't change a thing about my life as it was. "Rye, I wish you'd felt safe enough to tell me the truth when you first met me. I can't imagine what it must have been like for you at such a young age to lose your parents, and I'm glad that Aunt Rowena provided you a safe home when you needed one."

Sometimes I forget that you're the nice one in the family.

"Thank you, Raven." Rye reached down and grabbed his coffee cup. "I need to get back to the job I was working on at a house over near the bay. If it's all right with you, I'd like to sit down and talk some more about what Rowena has been through since your grandmother left the coven. I'm not going to make excuses for her behavior, but I think what I've found can help you and your mother understand my mom a bit better."

What Rowena has been through? Let me tell you—

I held up my hand to stave off Leo and my mother's two cents regarding the longstanding family feud. I'd learned a long time ago that there were three sides to every story. Aunt Rowena hadn't been able to forgive until it had been too late, but was it really ever too late to make amends?

Do you really want me to answer that?

"I'd like that, Rye. There's been too much bad blood thus far, and it's time we cleared that up."

I've clearly failed at teaching you how to be resolute when the situation warrants. I'll have to write that down in our learning lessons. I have a certain squirrel in mind that you can practice our offensive spells on, too.

Rye had taken maybe two steps when he abruptly stopped and turned back around, a cautious look on his face. I tensed, not knowing what else might be thrown my way.

"If I've learned anything by sitting back and observing how you and Leo do things, then I have no doubt the two of you are going to try to find out who killed Kevin Paul." Rye shook his head as if he didn't approve of our little side business. "Be careful. We don't know the nature of these people, and the last thing we need is to call attention to ourselves. I'm sure we can all agree on that."

He's not so bad, after all.

For once, my mother and Heidi remained quiet as Rye finally walked away in the same direction that Aunt Rowena had gone with the intention of getting out of Dodge. The thing of it was, I loved this place. I adored being a part of the Paramour Bay community, and soon Heidi would be calling this coastal town home, as well. No murderer should be left to roam the streets of our fair town unpunished.

Don't say it.

I was definitely going to say it, because my mother and Heidi both seemed to be weighing Rye's advice. The scale clearly wasn't going in my direction.

"It looks like we have a murder to solve, ladies and gent."

You just had to say it, didn't you?

Eight

"Aren't we taking a chance of running into Liam or Jack by doing this?" Heidi whispered, looking back over her shoulder to make sure no one had seen us head back toward the hive of well-used campers.

The area we were walking through was across the open field of the park. It was a short walk from the carnival at the edge of the street. There was a service road along the backside of the park with trees on either side to provide shade for the campsites the city usually rented out to the public. In this case, all the campsites had been reserved for the carnival's trucks, trailers, and a long string of campers used by the employees as their quarters while traveling from town to town throughout the carnival season.

You realize that we're entering Skippy territory, right? All I'm saying is be on the lookout...you never know when there could be an impending attack.

"If we do, just let me do the talking," Heidi insisted, knowing me so well. "The last time you tried to talk us out of a situation, you only made it sound worse."

You do have a bad habit of making a minor situation into something best described as critical.

"Buttons mentioned that Clara was staying inside Kevin's trailer," I murmured back, carefully searching the trailers for the one that had a skull and crossbones decal on the door. Mom had somehow managed to get a carnival worker to chit-chat about the murder, which technically wasn't too much of a feat considering that was all anyone was talking about since it happened, and she had somehow obtained the identifying information we needed to access Kevin Paul's personal belongings. "Maybe she's still there. It will make it easier to borrow an object of his to cast the remembrance spell."

Borrow? He's dead, Raven. I'm pretty sure he doesn't have any further need of his belongings. Unless, of course, he had an extra coffin lying around in his camper that he would need back.

Leo had followed us this far, but his job was to keep a lookout for Liam or Jack. It wouldn't benefit anyone for them to see us snatching something from the victim's camper, resulting in Heidi needing to come up with a plausible cover story.

Stop the bus! Back up the train! I think I just spotted Skippy underneath one of those campers over there.

"Leo, leave the squirrels alone. None of them are out to get you," I scolded him, not having time for one of his make-believe battles with the local wildlife. "We need to focus on finding Kevin Paul's murderer."

That's what I've been trying to tell you, Raven. There's a very real possibility the culprit could be those squirrels. Who knows what kind of strange squirrel pelt-smuggling conspiracy Kevin Paul was involved with before he came to Paramour Bay? They may have had a bounty on his head.

"...check on you in a bit," a woman called out, having

opened the door of a camper around thirty feet in front of us. Lo and behold, there was a decal of skull and crossbones right there in the middle of the door, just like the ones on a Jolly Roger pirate flag. Well, we'd definitely found Kevin Paul's camper. "Drink some of that tea I bought you from that place in town. The old guy doesn't know anything about tea, but my grandmother always said that chamomile with a dollop of newly harvested honey calmed the soul. The fresh honey was hard to find, but Rhonda had some on hand. See you after my shift."

My heart warmed at the thought of Olive going into town to buy Clara some tea from my shop for so many reasons. Heidi would have done the same for me, plus it meant that my tea shop was getting a little love from the carnival workers. I made a mental note to add a source of local honey to my list of items to keep in my inventory, and I honestly don't know why I hadn't thought of that before. It seemed so obvious now that I thought about it.

My BFF isn't getting any love from anyone, it seems. In his defense, his expertise does lie in rare premium catnip variations instead of tea blends. Few people know that there are over two hundred and fifty varieties of the catnip genus.

Heidi, Leo, and I watched as Olive quietly closed the door to Kevin Paul's camper, fully believing that she'd see us right away. I'd even stepped behind Heidi, seeing as she was the one who agreed to come up with the required cover story. Instead, Olive reached for her phone that was inside the grey apron she had tied around her waist. Her fingers flew across the keys, making me wonder just who she was texting in such a flurry.

"Hey, there," Heidi called out lightheartedly, but sooner than I'd expected. Olive practically dropped her phone at the startling interruption, finally clutching the device to her chest.

She was older than I would have expected, but maybe I was basing that on Button's age. Granted, I didn't know what he looked like underneath all that face paint, but he acted and spoke as if he were in his forties and not all that old. "We were looking for Bulldog."

Bulldog?

Raven, did my short-term memory loss just kick in? Is Heidi talking about a man with the nickname of Bulldog or an actual bulldog? I don't remember seeing one of those genetic misfits and serial droolers around here, but then again, Skippy has been messing with me. I've been quite distracted. I wouldn't put it past him to dognap an overzealous breed of dog to use as a mount.

"Bulldog is probably manning the hot dog stand, right now," Olive said cautiously, taking us in from head to toe. Her wary gaze didn't miss a thing, especially Leo, who had decided to plop himself in the grass beside me. "What are you doing back here? This area is restricted for use by carnival employees only. No visitors allowed."

"Bulldog told me to meet him back here for his relish recipe," Heidi shared, even rubbing her hands together in delight. "He said he'd part with it for fifty bucks, cold cash. I was so excited that I forgot to ask him which camper was his."

Olive was probably in her late fifties, with weathered skin that showed just how much time she must have spent in the sun over the years. Her golden blonde hair even had the sun-bleached ends. From where we were standing, it looked as if her eyes were bloodshot, but that could have been from crying over the death of her coworker.

Or she could have been lighting up a—

"I didn't mean to eavesdrop, but I overheard you say you were in town at the tea shop," I said with a forced smile, cutting off the direction Leo's thoughts had taken. I wanted to be truthful with this woman, but I wasn't sure she'd talk to us. We were outsiders, and seeing as Clara was her friend, it stood to reason that Kevin had been, too. "I happen to own *Tea, Leaves & Eves*. I'm glad we had some chamomile on hand for your friend. We heard what happened with Kevin Paul. You have our deepest sympathies for your loss."

Olive continued to regard us suspiciously, but Leo meowed at just the right moment. He made it seem as if we were harmless, which we were. Well, sort of. If you discounted my ability to hurl huge energy balls at opponents during a battle. Her shoulders relaxed just a bit, and she gave us a nod in appreciation. She had no idea that Leo had just complained about a yellow jacket that had suddenly flown past his ear.

"Clara is still pretty upset," Olive divulged, tucking her cell phone back inside her apron. "She and Kevin had just started dating a few weeks ago, and she really thought that he was the one, you know? By the way, you have a pretty nice shop."

"Thank you," I replied, grappling for something else to say. Nothing came to mind.

Par for the course. You could have used the opportunity to ask the woman outright if she thought Elroy Simpson was capable of murder.

"Well, I'd best get to work. Bulldog's camper is three down and two over on the opposite side. Can't miss it. He put a huge hot dog decal on the door."

"Thanks," Heidi said, but I wasn't ready to finish the conversation. "I—"

"I'm actually dating our local sheriff here in Paramour Bay," I confessed, wincing internally when I sounded as if I was boasting. I wasn't, and I quickly attempted to rectify my statement. "I overheard him say that some guy named Elroy

Simpson might be responsible for your friend's death. Do you think any of the residents have anything to worry about?"

Wow. Subtle. Real subtle.

Heidi was also giving me a wide-eyed look that told me I might have overstepped my bounds, but I blamed Leo. He was the one who'd put the idea into my head.

"It's all anyone's been talking about, but I know Elroy personally. I worked with him for years, and I can tell you that he wouldn't have harmed a hair on a puppy dog's head."

What about a cat? Does he have a grudge against full-grown cats?

Olive didn't look happy that some things were being said about an old colleague. She was beginning to fidget and shift her weight from one leg to another.

"I'm sorry," I apologized, truly regretting even bringing up Kevin Paul's name. "It's none of our business, and I didn't mean to accuse anyone when we don't know the people involved. It also wasn't nice of me to repeat secondhand gossip that I'd overheard."

There you go again, being too nice.

"Look, Clara really liked Kevin. I didn't blame him when George made the decision to hire him and fire Elroy. We're used to these kinds of things happening around here, but usually a newb is given a three-month probation period before he or she is hired on full-time. I don't know why Kevin didn't have to go through one, the same as the rest of us, but there was some talk that he was related to George somehow. You know how it is. Blood is thicker than water. It doesn't matter anymore. Kevin is dead, but you can take it to heart that no one in this town has anything to worry about, because I know that Elroy didn't kill him."

"Olive?"

93

The door to Kevin's camper had opened and revealed a younger woman, but still one who clearly spent a lot of time in the sunshine. She was rather petite with her mousy brunette hair drawn high in a ponytail. She was a bit pale underneath her tan, and her nose was red from crying.

Did you see that? That annoying yellow jacket flew right past her and into the trailer. I thought I was having a bad day. That thing is going to sting her for sure.

"Is everything okay?" Clara asked, holding the cup of tea Olive had made her close to her chest.

"Yes, sugar." Olive waved a hand protectively to indicate that Clara should go back inside. "Just some locals who Bulldog promised his relish recipe to, so nothing to worry about. Go back inside. I'm late enough as it is, and Seymour is going to say I owe him for not swapping on time. You know how that turned out last time."

Seymour sounds like my kind of guy. I wonder if he can help with my squirrel problem.

Olive continued to stare at us long enough that I realized she didn't want to leave Clara standing outside of Kevin Paul's trailer. Talk about loyalty. I easily related, and I really needed an object owned by Kevin to cast the spell. Neither of these women had a clue that I was only trying to help them, and I was coming up blank for an excuse that would garner me such an item.

"I hate to bother you," Heidi exclaimed, throwing her hands up in the air as if she were helpless when she was anything but. "You wouldn't happen to have a piece of paper and a pencil I could use to write down Bulldog's recipe, would you? I left my purse at home because we were going to be riding some of the rides."

I loved Heidi's creativity in situations like these.

She does have a gift.

"Yeah, I'm sure there's something inside. Give me half a second," Clara said, using a tissue to wipe her nose. She gave Olive a small smile of reassurance. "Go. Seriously, I'm fine. I'll give these young ladies a pad and pencil, and then I'm going to go lie down for a bit."

Olive finally relented, slowly walking away toward the carnival rides and whichever game Seymour was currently manning. I admired her devotion to Clara, and I would do what I could to bring both of them closure. Solving this crime might have started out with my wish to protect the supernatural, but it was now much more than that.

You're getting all sentimental, Raven. You know that I don't like having my heartstrings tugged on. In case you didn't notice, you've been yanking on them like they were lanyards hanging from your favorite church bells at Notre Dame, Miss Hunchback.

"Here you go," Clara said softly, having reached just inside the camper door. Sure enough, she had a small pad and pencil in hand. "Don't worry about bringing it back. Kevin won't be needing it anymore. He'd use it to figure the odds on the horses."

Clara didn't have to say why, and my heart squeezed tight with the grief she must be going through today. Without another word, she quietly closed the camper door.

I've got something in my eye, just in case you were wondering why I'm blinking so rapidly.

"Now what do we do?" Heidi asked, holding up the objects that would hopefully lead to Kevin Paul's murderer being put behind bars. "Can you cast the spell here?"

"No, I'm going to need the right spell components." I did have an idea, though. I took the pad and pencil, writing down the ingredients I'd need from memory. I'd done this particular spell before. Once I had everything listed, I took my cell phone out of my skirt pocket and snapped a picture. "I'll send a text to Mom, letting her know we got what we needed. She can use my car to drive to the cottage and give Ted the list of the additional items we'll need him to gather."

Suppose you can pull her away from Beetle. I'm still not ready to discuss what went down this morning between them. Can we keep avoiding that topic for now? My stomach is finally settling. Let's revisit the subject only if they end up having that dinner they talked about this morning.

I wasn't going to argue with Leo's logic on that particular subject. I couldn't wrap my mind around my mother actually agreeing to share a meal with Beetle, either. It made me wonder if she was up to something. Possibly recruiting herself a spy. If I found even an inkling of evidence that she was going to use Beetle in some deceitful fashion, I'd immediately put an end to it. Beetle was too sweet a man to get caught up in one of my mother's underhanded schemes.

"Bulldog? Really?"

"I met him when I was looking for the wine your mother wanted at lunch, and we got to talking about New York," Heidi responded with a smile. "One thing led to another, and the next thing I know...he's offering up his relish recipe."

"You never cease to amaze me."

Me, either. Do you think there's a spell where we can turn her into a hot-looking feline?

"Listen, let me call my realtor and see if she can move up the time on the next house listing," Heidi suggested, pulling her own phone out of the back pocket of her jeans. "It sounds like we're going to need all the time we can get later tonight."

While Heidi was on the phone, I noticed that the palm of

my hand had begun tingling sometime in the last five minutes. I'd thought maybe it was because I was writing on a piece of paper that belonged to a dead guy, but now I wasn't so sure. The hairs on the back of my neck were standing at attention, and heat began to pool in my palm.

Someone's watching us, Raven. And it's not Skippy.

Leo vanished into thin air. I cautiously waited for him to return, taking the time to look around at all the campers. There were a lot of places for someone to hide. Unfortunately, Heidi completed her phone call before Leo could reappear.

"Where did Leo go?" Heidi asked, searching the area for any sign of my familiar. "What happened?"

"Someone was watching us," I said warily, suddenly having the urge to rejoin the carnival where we'd be surrounded by witnesses. "Let's go. Leo will catch up with us."

It was one thing to stay on the outskirts of this type of investigation, providing Liam or Jack with useful information to help solve a murder. After all, I could easily protect us if something went wrong in my immediate vicinity. Regrettably, Heidi couldn't do the same if we were separated.

"Did you happen to catch Olive mentioning that there were rumors that Kevin was related to George?" Heidi asked, as aware of our surroundings as I was now that my palm was practically burning. I closed my hand into a fist, hoping to ease the uncomfortable sensation, but the tingling only became worse at the mention of George. Was he the one responsible for Kevin's death? "Do you think that was mentioned to Liam or Jack?"

"Probably, but it couldn't hurt to bring it up to them in conversation." I breathed a little easier the closer we got to the loud sounds of the carnival rides and the growing afternoon crowd. Unfortunately, nothing seemed to be easing the heat in my palm. "Heidi, I can't put a finger on it, but I've got a bad feeling about this murder mystery."

Heidi didn't immediately respond, and I glanced her way to see why. She hadn't stopped walking, but her blue eyes were wide with shock. I followed her gaze to find that a large group of people was gathered around the carousel, but that's not what caught her eye. It was the fact that yellow crime scene tape now surrounded one of the most popular children's attractions that had apparently been shut down for the day. At least, that's what the sign in front of the ride stated.

"Look," Heidi said, pointing a finger past the crowd. Liam and Jack were talking with a forensic person who held an evidence bag in his hand.

There you are!

Leo sounded a bit out of breath. He'd come running out from behind one of the game booths to make his sudden appearance less conspicuous. His fur jiggled with each step of his jog.

I couldn't find anyone watching us from any of the campers, but good ol' Olive might not be so good, after all. Give me a second. I can't breathe. What idiot said running was good for your health? I'm pretty sure my lungs aren't supposed to feel like they're ready to explode.

"Raven, did you hear that?" Heidi wasn't referring to Leo, but instead one of the carnival workers who had been talking to another colleague. "They think the police found a wallet of the man who used to work here. They must be talking about Elroy Simpson."

Could it be that simple? There was more and more evidence piling up against Mr. Simpson, from him being spotted in the area to his wallet being found maybe fifteen yards from the scene of the crime. By the time Heidi and I made it back to the cottage to cast the spell, Liam and Jack might very well have apprehended the killer themselves.

Don't bank on it. Olive didn't go relieve Seymour like she said she was going to when she left the campers. Instead, she went to George Mertes' trailer.

I knelt down to the ground to pet Leo, giving others the appearance that I was showering affection on my furbaby.

"Why would that be suspicious?" I whispered, scratching behind Leo's ear. Even though he could read my mind, I still had a hard time not talking to him when I wanted to know something. "George is Olive's boss, right? It doesn't seem so out of place that she'd want to talk to him about being late for her shift."

Scratch my shoulder blade while you're at it. There. Yeah, that hits the spot.

Loud purrs of satisfaction almost overtook the murmuring of the gathered crowd in front of us. Leo practically fell onto his side in relief after I'd finished giving him a small massage where the squirrel had landed on his shoulders.

"Leo?"

What? Did you see a squirrel somewhere?

I closed my eyes and counted to ten, telling myself over and over that it wasn't his fault that he had short-term memory loss. My all-too-brief moment of attempted composure was gone the moment Heidi grabbed my arm and yanked me off the ground.

"Olive is talking to Bulldog," Heidi muttered in disbelief, turning away so that her back was to them. "Bulldog and I talked about relish recipes, but he never said for me to meet him at his camper. Olive is going to know that we lied if we don't intercede."

Olive? Oh, I remember now. Wow! How could I forget some-

thing like that? I might need to stop in at the tea shop for some of Beetle's premium catnip snacks. I've gone too long without a booster buzz. Anyway, I overheard Olive tell George that they needed to hide the evidence! That can only mean one thing, Raven.

"Leo found out that Olive and George might have killed Kevin Paul," I whispered to Heidi, finishing Leo's assumption. "Heidi, if that's the case, we need to prove they did and then find evidence to give Liam and Jack reason to suspect them."

You two can handle this case from here on out. I'm going back to the shop for some catnip and inspirational enlightenment. I'm going to need all the help I can get if I'm going to take down Skippy in this year's squirrel versus cat battle. I know just the weapon, too—Rye Dolgiram, my new personal warlock slash fix-it man.

Nine

Raven, do something about your mother. She's driving me insane.

I couldn't take the time right now to delve into what my mother had done to make Leo so angry. My current situation had me in a bit of a bind, and any indication that Leo had followed me into the police station would have Liam thinking that stumbling over another dead body had sent me over the edge. It was too bad that Aunt Rowena's earlier spell had worn off.

"How did the second showing go?" Liam asked, walking in front of me as he led the way back to his office. I couldn't help but smile, and he'd immediately noticed. "What?"

"You still take time to ask me about my day when I know how incredibly busy you are," I replied, walking right up to him and wrapping my arms around his neck. His brown eyes had small creases at the sides, telling me that the stress of the case was taking its toll on his normally benevolent outlook. "Heidi liked the first house better, but there's still one to look at on tomorrow morning's schedule before she heads back to

101

the city. She wanted to squeeze in as many showings as the realtor had available. Now, is there anything I can do for you? It's almost five o'clock. Do you want me to go over to the diner to pick you up something to eat?"

Now we're on the same page. Just so you know, a small snack would have sufficed. But nooo, your mother couldn't allow Beetle to acknowledge my presence. I even tried yelling at the top of my voice. You know what she told him? That I must have gotten into a scrap with a squirrel, ill-tempered as I was. She purposefully used Skippy's vendetta against me. Raven, I'll have you know—it is possible to have withdrawal symptoms from catnip. I know you can't see me right now, but my paw is oddly shaking. I think I'm beginning to go into detox.

Eileen was busy manning the phones, apparently getting numerous tips on Elroy Simpson's whereabouts from residents and tourists alike. News had made the rounds that Elroy Simpson's wallet had been found near the crime scene, and everyone and their mother had sworn they'd seen him at various places around town. I wasn't so sure that was the case, given the exchange that Leo had overheard between Olive and George.

That's old news. Right now, your mother has Beetle cooped up in the back of the storage room doing only the supernatural knows what behind those beads! He won't pay a lick of attention to me, and I'm in dire need of my pipe. This situation needs to be rectified, posthaste.

"I appreciate the offer, but I've got too much on my plate right now." Liam rested his warm hands on my hips as he leaned back against the desk. The palm of my hand wasn't the only thing that sensed when danger was near. Right now, it was as if I could literally feel the tension radiating through Liam's body. "Listen, what are your plans tonight?"

Feeding me, because obviously I'm going to miss out on my

snack. I'll be skin and bones by the time we get home. My empty stomach will be rubbing on my backbone by then.

I could easily hear the concern in Liam's tone for my well-being. Something had happened in the investigation that Heidi, Leo, and I weren't aware of, and it must be a doozy. As for Leo, trust me, he was far from turning into a skeleton.

"Heidi is out front waiting for me. We were thinking of heading back to the cottage for a bit, and then we were going to take Mom to the carnival this evening to maybe catch some of that live folk music," I replied with a slight question to my tone, searching Liam's brown eyes for any sign that those plans might be changing in the next few seconds. "Has something important happened?"

Yes, something really important has happened. I've been trying to explain to you that my stomach is shrinking with every second that passes by on the clock. If I didn't know better, I'd think you were in cahoots with Skippy to starve me to death.

"We believe there's a clandestine drug ring operating inside the carnival, which most likely resulted in Kevin Paul being killed when he did or said something he shouldn't have," Liam confided in me quietly, his unease with the situation evident. "We're not sure whether Paul was in on it or if he stumbled across something he wasn't supposed to see. My first instinct was to close down the whole show and alert the Feds, because of the interstate nature of the crimes...maybe even the DEA. Jack and his lieutenant have someone on the inside, so I'm left with the lid on this whole mess until the carnival packs up Monday morning. Ultimately, it's their call as to what they want to do. Truthfully, I'd rather you, your family, and friend stay away from the place for the rest of the weekend."

Drugs? It had never crossed my mind that drugs had been involved with Kevin Paul's murder, but now some of the pieces began to fall into place. George and Olive had to be in on the side action. They were too close to the daily operations not to have noticed something that big going on around them. Why else would Olive have run to George after finding Heidi and me snooping around the campers, especially after I mentioned that I was dating the sheriff? Maybe that hadn't been the best tactic, after all.

Liam is wiser than I give him credit for, and you know how I hate to agree with the man. We stay away from the carnival, remaining inside where we can smoke all the catnip we could possibly desire, and then come up with a brilliant plan to annihilate the entire squirrel population of Paramour Bay in one fell swoop. Magnificent!

Liam had no idea that I planned to go home after this brief visit in order to cast a spell to confirm that George, Olive, or even Elroy was involved with the murder of Kevin Paul. Liam's investigative work had obviously produced more vital information than anything Heidi and I had managed to find, but Leo was constantly reminding me that it was Liam's job to investigate crimes in the first place. I didn't feel so bad, given my amateur status. Liam took his job seriously, learned from the best of the best back when he was with the NYPD, and made a darn fine sheriff of our little town. With that said, it didn't mean I couldn't help close this case with a nice big red bow tied on top of the case file.

Have you learned nothing over the last six months? When standing on a boat, avoid rocking it back and forth. If not, someone is sure to get wet. I, for one, hate water.

"This wasn't how I pictured our first Spring Festival." I lowered my hands until my palms were resting on his chest. I didn't feel right about keeping information from him, so I decided to fess up about Buttons. "You should know that

Mom felt bad for a clown this morning, so she invited him to have breakfast with us. He seemed nice enough."

What is wrong with you? Clowns aren't mentally stable, Raven. They harbor evil intentions. Everyone knows that, and I'm way past the point where I was unsure there was something majorly wrong with the way your brain functions.

"The investigation is focused on those individuals a little higher up in the organization, but there's a good chance it's trickled down to the other employees," Liam warned, basically confirming that he didn't trust anyone associated with the carnival. "Again, I think it's best if—"

Good gracious, my eyes!

"Liam?" Eileen asked, appearing in the open doorway. Her bright pink sweater with a white rabbit in the center of her chest was really hard to miss, but she was known for her penchant for holiday apparel. I'm pretty sure she even had rabbit earrings dangling from her earlobes, but it was really hard to adjust my eyesight away from the bright colored fabric. "Jack is on line one, and the mayor is on line two. I tried to explain to Mayor Sanders that now wasn't a good time, but he wouldn't take no for an answer."

"Thanks, Eileen."

Someone needs to put a warning label on that woman. Geez, she must be a hardcore rabbit fanatic.

I stepped back so that Liam could turn around and reach for his desk phone. He most likely wanted some privacy, but he motioned for me to remain in his office. I stepped to the window that faced the main thoroughfare through Paramour Bay, noting that there wasn't a parking spot to be had on River Bay. There was no sight of Heidi out front, so I figured she was keeping Eileen company in the outer office.

Can't you just tell Heidi to come with me to the tea shop?

She'll get me one of those baggies filled with Beetle's catnip treats. The ones he keeps in his shirt pocket underneath his cardigan. Unless he's no longer wearing his cardigan and shirt at this stage. It's entirely possible, you know.

Leo wasn't playing fair. The thought of Beetle and my mother together was just flat out wrong on so many levels, but I doubt that Mom would actually go down that treacherous path. Beetle wasn't her type, and she had very hard and fast rules when it came to the residents of Paramour Bay.

You know, now that we've been reassured that Rye didn't kill that carnival worker, I think it's safe to say we can send your mother packing before you get a new sister out of the ordeal. On the other hand, I'm relatively sure that's impossible with her age, but we do have to take into consideration that she is a witch. Weirder things have happened.

"...mayor is on the other line, Jack. I'm still not comfortable with setting up this sting when so many of the residents will be at the carnival tonight. Are you sure your source is reliable?"

I've made an executive decision. I'm going back over to the tea shop to evict Regina. Wish me luck. I might need to burn my eyes out when I'm done. This is me, taking one for the team.

Leo didn't wait around for me to disagree. I could sense that he'd left, but I also had no doubt that my mother would stay to help with tonight's spell. I'd successfully done this particular incantation a couple of times without issue, so it wasn't as if she needed to worry about me catching the house on fire and causing Leo's tail to go numb again. Mom would stay simply to see how far I've come in our craft and probably offer up an evaluation that I could do without at this point. I was well beyond needing my mother to sign my report card.

"As a matter of fact, Raven is here with me now."

Jack must have asked about Heidi. I faced Liam and walked toward his desk, where there were quite a few files. He was a neat freak, so the manila folders most likely had to do with the case. Was Buttons working as Jack's informant on the inside? Maybe Clara?

It was really hard to wait for Liam to finish up his call when a simple spell could solve the mystery of who killed Kevin Paul. I'd given Heidi the pad and pencil to hold onto while I finished talking with Liam, and it was time to use the objects we'd garnered from the victim's camper to identify the killer.

"Really? That's interesting to know." Liam didn't take his inquisitive dark gaze off me. My palm began to tingle, but this time without the warmth. Oh, this wasn't good. Heidi was the one who was quick on her feet. Me? Not so much. "Maybe she just likes friendly clowns."

Somehow, some way, Jack must have figured out Heidi and I had been talking to some of the carnival employees about the murder. What kind of believable excuse could I come up with when Liam finally had a chance to ask me why we were getting involved? I was coming up blank, so it was best if I just removed myself from the situation before it broke wide open.

I forced a smile and then made a motion with my hand that I was going to head out to let Liam finish up his phone conversation. My peacock skirt billowed around my knee-high boots as I made my way to the door. I'd almost made it past Liam when he snagged my hand, a small smirk on his lips.

"Jack found out about your breakfast with your new friend, Lyle Gafney," Liam informed me, holding the phone close to his chest. He still had another call to take, but relief was hot and fast as it traveled at the speed of light through my veins. We'd had breakfast with Buttons, whose real name must be Lyle Gafney. "You might want to warn Heidi that she's about to get a call from Jack."

Liam's grin faded, telling me that he really was worried about us getting in too deep.

"Raven, we aren't dealing with a crime of passion here. The rap sheets on the people we're looking into are very long and filled with very serious charges. We're dealing with some very dangerous individuals, but I have to trust that Jack and the state narcotics division know what they're doing. Please, just give me some peace of mind—stay at home tonight."

I nodded my agreement, not seeing why Heidi, my mother, and I would even need to leave the house at this point. Should the spell conjure up the identity of the person who killed Kevin Paul, I could somehow find another spell in the grimoire that would have me connect with Liam in some way to give him the information—maybe by a passing thought that I could plant inside his mind as Mother did with Heidi that one time. I've certainly read stranger things inside the family grimoire. Then again, that might be considered a total violation of the mind. I'd have to think on that one.

"We'll stay home," I assured him with every intention of keeping my promise. "Please call me with updates so that I'm not up all night worrying about you."

"Hey," Liam said softly, not releasing my hand. In fact, he tugged me toward him and stole a very sweet kiss. "I like it when you think about me."

"Oh, would you two lovebirds give that stuff up already? We're in public here," Heidi exclaimed facetiously, standing just outside the doorway with her hands on her hips. She impatiently blew at a blonde curl that had fallen into her face. "Let's go grab your mother before she gives Beetle a heart attack."

I didn't miss the way Liam arched his brow in question at

Heidi's last statement, but it was too long a story to get into, and he didn't have the time to hear it. I blew him a kiss and finally left him to take the call with the mayor that would no doubt put this entire office in a bad mood. Mayor Sanders didn't like it when any major crimes occurred on his watch, but particularly something of this magnitude.

"Why do you look so pale?" Heidi whispered to me after we waved our goodbyes to Eileen. The dispatcher was answering what sounded like numerous incoming calls, but the bright sweater somehow made things seem not so bad in comparison. I could now understand why she wore them. "Did something happen?"

"Drugs."

"Drugs?"

"Drugs," I confirmed, pushing open the glass door to the police station and stepping out onto the sidewalk. The warm sun was a little lower in the sky, but we still had some daylight left. "Kevin Paul might have been killed over trafficking drugs across state lines. It sounds like some sting is about to take place tonight, so we don't have any time to waste. Let's go find ourselves a killer."

Ten

"...don't have a say in who I get to spend my time with or who I don't, Leo."

Beetle is my primo catnip supplier, and what exactly do you think is going to happen when you go and break the poor man's heart?. From what I hear, you've already done it once before. Are such affairs of the heart mere gist for your relationship mill? Knowing you, you'll use your millstone to grind his soul to dust.

"You listen to me, *Benny*."

Leo's offended gasp echoed off the loft overhead at the way my mother stressed his real name from before he'd been...well, before he'd been unnaturally pulled back here after passing through death's threshold. I wasn't sure what to call his transformation through black necromancy magic, but it didn't matter at the moment. My mother had delivered a low blow. I wasn't worried in the least, though. Leo could certainly hold his own.

Ha! Listen to you, Regina? Not in this lifetime, nor the next! I'm not the one who packed my bags and let Rosemary down by...

My mother and Leo were currently in the living room of my cottage, arguing over the fact that my mom had indeed gone to dinner with Beetle. It was now going on seven o'clock in the evening, and she'd walked through the door only five minutes ago. Since then, it's been a knockdown, drag-out, all barrels blazing catfight.

"Aren't you going to do something, Miss Raven?"

"Nope," I quipped back to Ted, taking a sip of the wine Heidi had poured for us only moments before my mother arrived. I'd gotten used to these verbal exchanges, and it was best to let the fighting duo get their frustrations out now rather than when I was in the middle of something...like casting a spell. "They'll eventually get this out of their systems. They always do. I've got no dog in this fight."

Ted was standing while Heidi and I sat at the small island that separated the kitchen from the living room. We were all lined up on the stools facing the ongoing duel between witch and veteran familiar. I was positioned between Ted towering over me on the end and Heidi on the other side, reevaluating my previous answer after Leo had brought up Mom's decision to leave and divorce herself from witchcraft. She'd cut all ties to our family's legacy, but that wasn't entirely true, was it?

My mother had continued to secretly use magic in her own life after running off to the city. Her momentous decision was mostly designed to deprive me of my birthright and steal any chance I might have had to be a part of my grandmother's life.

Maybe I *should* bring this current argument to a halt before Leo or I say something we would all regret.

"Ted brought all the ingredients," Heidi pointed out with a small tilt of her wineglass toward a basket of herbs, roots, and rose petals that had been set in the middle of the coffee table.

"You've done this spell before. We don't have to wait for those two to draw blood. I'm not even sure they'd notice the floating petals and flickering flames of the candles."

Everything Heidi pointed out was true, but concentration did play a big part in casting incantations. Providing a distraction wasn't what either of them should be doing. Doing even a simple spell under these circumstances wasn't the wisest of choices. After all, I had been known to drop an inflection a time or two. Mother didn't have a tail, but her hair could turn white or her complexion could wither.

"They're making too much racket," I muttered, taking another sip of my wine. We all sucked in air when my mother brought up Leo's somewhat disheveled appearance. "They have to run out of insults and breath soon, right?"

I'd spoken too soon.

Leo began to point out that Mom hadn't truly left behind this way of life the day she'd departed for New York City. Her twisted departure had only hurt others with her selfish, defiant behavior. She technically didn't have the right to come back to town as if she owned the place and try to destroy what little of a relationship she'd left between Nan and me. It wasn't a surprise when his litany of sharp-ended points riled my mother to the juncture of taking that argument down another road.

Don't get me wrong.

Leo was right on every count.

Mom *had* chosen to abandon Nan and our lineage, all the while keeping my past under wraps for her own selfish reasons. I hadn't known about the Marigolds' history and the good work we could do in this world. Using my abilities to make the holistic blends with a sprinkle of magic helped the residents of Paramour Bay, and that alone made me feel as if I was fully contributing to my new community.

Nan had left me the tea shop, which concealed the true reason she'd opened up such a business in a small town. It afforded her the leisure of using small amounts of white magic without any real threat of being caught by the townsfolk. As for the quaint cottage on the edge of town, she'd made it appear eerie enough on the outside so that no one really wanted to make social calls. Entering such a private domain opened a witch up to the vulnerability of being discovered in her lair.

As for the interior, well, the modern décor was all Nan. I loved what she'd done with the place.

I wouldn't technically have called Nan materialistic, but she certainly did like the finer things in her domestic life. The cottage was a one-story abode with a loft that was accessed by an ornately carved spiral staircase that appeared to be cut from a single massive black oak. The bedroom was located above the kitchen and could be observed from the front entrance.

Nan had added splashes of bright colors everywhere, yet the living room furniture was a hive of natural colors that matched the neutral cream paint on the walls. There was even a large river stone fireplace with a black oak mantle, but it was the intricately carved hardwood coffee table that was the heart of this home. The elaborate yet obscure carvings had been hand-carved by skilled craftsmen, and there were secret drawers hidden in every nook and cranny of the live oak. It was where she'd kept the family grimoire, and rightly so—the protection wards cast on the coffee table were like none other I'd ever seen.

Not that I'd seen a lot in the six months I'd been here since I'd found out I was a witch.

Heidi and I both startled when Ted abruptly stepped forward toward the battling duo, which wasn't much of a stretch considering he was six feet and six inches tall. His black suit was spotless without even the slightest piece of lint to be found on the pristine fabric. He stuck his two index fingers into his mouth and blew, creating a piercing whistle that had my mother and Leo clutching their ears, along with Heidi and me.

Did I fail to mention that Ted was a dead ringer for Lurch from *The Addams Family*?

Literally.

He had previously been part of a wax museum's collection.

Odd, I know, but Paramour Bay had a wax museum that could be observed right as one drove into town. Nan had gotten the bright idea that bringing wax figures to life could make her life easier. I'm pretty sure she'd taken such drastic measures because she was lonely and wanted a little more companionship than her surly familiar.

"There is no need to fight," Ted declared, a frown on his rather chiseled features. "Stop this childish nonsense. Right now."

He tended to talk in short sentences, but that might have to do with the fact that he didn't have a brain or any other vital organs. At least, I don't think he did in the sense that we had them.

Tell that giant grey crayon to mind his own business. There is a higher calling before us, a need to fight and rectify this situation. Regina, I forbid you to date Beetle.

"What is Leo saying?" Ted asked, his frown still in place as he turned to me for an explanation.

Seeing as Ted was supernatural but not a witch or warlock, he couldn't hear what Leo was saying. I didn't need to answer, though, because my mother told Leo exactly where he could go after he'd attempted to tell her how to live her life.

"What is wrong with someone needing love?"

Ted's question—more importantly, the way he'd phrased it—had everyone immediately falling silent, even Leo. He'd been on the arm of the couch while my mother had taken the over-stuffed chair, giving both of them the ability to lean forward in their attempt to make their points.

"Who said anything about love?" my mother asked in disbelief, a bit of shock glistening in those green eyes of hers. "Ted, it was only dinner."

"A dinner that might eventually lead to love."

Am I hearing this right? I don't have time for this wax giant to get philosophical, Raven. I'm not done making my point.

"I'm not a fan of Ms. Regina, either."

Heidi choked on her wine at Ted's somewhat flippant interpretation.

"I beg your pardon?" my mother snapped back, clearly outraged over Ted's opinion of her. I wasn't sure why, considering he'd only been in existence for ten or eleven years, well after she'd left town. I'm certain Ted had heard quite the earful from Nan regarding her only daughter and the choices she'd made with her life. "I will have you know that—"

He has a valid point, Regina. Let it go.

It was a good thing I hadn't taken a sip of wine, or else it would have been all over my skirt. Ted had assumed Leo had said something insulting toward my mother, and he hadn't given me a chance to interpret.

"Does that mean Miss Regina shouldn't find love?"

I quickly caught Heidi up to speed with a whisper, not wanting to interrupt Ted's deeply held opinion on the matter of love. He might not have a lot of common sense, but I did have to give him credit. There were times when I truly believed he had more of an understanding of humanity than the rest of us put together.

"We are built for companionship."

What are we? Chopped liver? Raven, I'm failing to see the point here.

"We all need love."

I had to give Ted his due. He often didn't speak in this manner, but it was clearly an important subject he'd apparently given a great deal of thought to. Leo had pulled back slightly off the arm of the couch, as if he were surprised that Ted could be so sentimental. It wasn't really surprising, given the fact that Ted was in love with a mannequin at the boutique store in town. The owner, Mindy, chalked it up to Ted being a little bit eccentric.

"It's nice to hold someone's hand," Ted continued with what I was afraid would become a permanent frown. His dark eyes swept over Leo. "Or paw, in your case."

Ted didn't seem to understand why Leo and my mother wouldn't agree with him. He paused with each sentence, so it wasn't as if they weren't being given ample time to do so. His thought process took things down into their simplest forms, and he had the ability to strike at the heart of the matter with just a few succinct words.

I actually agreed with him, and I didn't want to leave him hanging.

"Ted, you're right. Everyone should experience love in their lives. Having someone to laugh with at all our silly jokes, cry with us when we're sad, and grow old with us so we have a hand to hold when it comes time for the last farewell," I replied softly, resting a hand on his stiff arm. Nan hadn't thought this part through, had she? Bringing to life an inanimate object, only to have him be alone. Sure, he had us...as Leo had so eloquently stated a little bit ago. Having Liam in my life had me seeing things differently, and maybe it was time to consider giving Ted a companion after we solved this current murder mystery. "Mom, we won't say another word if Beetle is someone you'd truly like to get reacquainted with from your youth."

Who is this we you speak of? You and Heidi? Have you got Skippy in your pocket? I could see him taking your side in this. It's surely not me you're talking about, because that is not where I was headed with my previous conversation.

"I'd like to put a caveat on that statement, though," I warned, wanting to be clear about the line between personal and professional, while also ensuring our witchcraft abilities were kept safe. After all, Beetle was my employee. "Mother, you've warned me numerous times about my relationship with Liam, and the fact that I even hired Beetle in the first place was a matter of concern, and also about my choice to live here in Paramour Bay from the start. You have to promise me that you'll take your own warnings to heart."

Wise choice, though I'm not sure there was enough threatening tone laced in your voice. Maybe you should try it again with some possible punishments thrown in.

"I'd say that's a compromise on all sides, wouldn't you?" Heidi pointed out happily.

Leo was regarding Ted with wariness, almost as if my familiar was weighing the advice given by a so-called wax golem. Heidi began to refill our glasses as if I'd somehow reversed roles with my mother, but she actually appeared to be giving my opinion a bit of thought on the matter.

"I'll admit that I was flirting with Beetle at first to rile up you and Leo," Mom replied, looking down at her nails as if she'd suddenly found them somewhat interesting. She cleared her throat before continuing, telling me that whatever she was about to say wasn't going to be easy for her to admit. "But there's something rather...charming about a man my own age. He doesn't care what other people think of me, and I find that quite refreshing. A couple more dinners couldn't hurt to get caught up on old times, but you know that I would never— ever—jeopardize what you've built here. I might not agree with all of your choices, but I've come to accept that you're a grown woman who makes her own decisions."

"Here, here," Heidi exclaimed, raising a glass in Ted's direction, seeing as he was the one who'd gotten us this far. "To seeing the silver lining of possibilities."

Ted still had a grimace on his rather square face, evidently not quite sure we'd truly understood what he had been attempting to convey. I would completely disagree, especially seeing as Leo's left eye was practically glued to the utterly simplistic yet oddly insightful giant. I guess I'd never stopped to think about Leo and his personal life. Was there a female cat or another familiar that had crossed his path recently? Was there more to that magical fairy lipstick mark on his fur than I initially thought?

What? None of your business, missy. I'm done talking about this sappy stuff. First, you go and hook up with the sheriff, of all people. Then you spill the one secret we in the supernatural world hold sacred to Heidi. That alone could get us turned into toads by the coven. Was that enough? Noooo. Now you expect me to accept that your mother is dating my best high-end catnip supplier, all due to a foolishly sentimental speech given by an oversized waxed crayon. And lest we forget, we now have a new cousin in our neck of the woods who just happens to be a warlock who calls your great-aunt Mother.

"Does Leo need a hug?" Heidi whispered teasingly, twisting around to set her wine glass on the counter before she stood and made her way over to Leo. "Come here, you little furball."

You tell Heidi that it's not going to work this time. I'm not going to be cuddled into shutting up about this train wreck. This is a dire situation, and one we need to rectify posthaste, if not sooner. A simple warning will not do under these circumstances. There must be consequences.

Leo continued to squirm in protest, and he even tried to turn his head the other way when Heidi finally scooped him up in her arms. She knew exactly how to get him to cave with a gentle nuzzle to his neck. I could practically hear him break out into a purr from my seat on the stool.

We might be able to deal with your mother's catting around tomorrow.

"Could we please get on with casting this spell, helping your fetching sheriff solve his case, and allowing me to have an early breakfast with a dear old friend?" my mother inquired with a roll of her eyes at how easily Leo had acquiesced to Heidi's cuddling advances. "I need my beauty sleep."

Heidi quickly prevented Leo from hurling another insult my mother's way by scratching underneath his chin. She settled back on the couch with a relenting Leo in her arms, so I snatched up her wine and walked it over to her.

"I'll leave you to your business, Miss Raven." Ted usually didn't stay around for the spellcasting, and it appeared he was back to his terse sentence structure. "Goodnight, ladies."

"Thank you for gathering the ingredients, Ted," I called out as he walked stiffly to the front door. Seriously, he never asked for anything. One of these days, I was going to figure out a way to bring that mannequin to life for him. He was absolutely right when he said that people shouldn't grow old alone.

Then again, would Ted ever grow old? It was something I needed to genuinely consider. "Goodnight."

I took my usual seat on the oversized burgundy pillow I kept between the coffee table and hearth. The heat on my back was very comforting as I began to separate the components needed for the spell in their various pestles. I could already sense the energy of the earth surging and building beneath me.

"Well, I figure Liam and Jack have already identified the individuals within the carnival who are trafficking drugs," I reasoned, taking the time to light the candles that Mom had set out before getting into an argument with Leo. "Otherwise, they wouldn't be conducting some sort of drug sting tonight. Right?"

"I'd say that's right," Heidi agreed with a nod, casting a glance in my mother's direction. "Mrs. M?"

"Agreed." Regina leaned forward and moved one of the pestles closer to me, forming a more perfectly symmetric semi-circle. "We're specifically looking for who killed Mr. Paul so that we can be sure he or she is arrested with these same individuals involved in the sting. There is something to be said for justice in human terms, so let's not waste any more time. Raven?"

If there's not enough evidence to arrest them, we can always give Rowena a call. I don't care for her, but she definitely has the ability to turn almost anyone into a toad.

Leo had thrown that suggestion out almost indifferently, completely immersed in Heidi's affection. We weren't turning anyone into toads—truthfully, I wasn't even sure that could happen regardless of the old wives' tales. I was simply gathering information for Liam, so that this town could once again breathe a little easier knowing that the killer had been caught and thrown behind bars.

I purposefully took a deep breath and made myself settle on the pillow. I was well-acquainted with this spell, and I had no worries that we would have the answers we sought in a matter of minutes. Leo had been lying in Heidi's arms, but his head popped up, and his bulging left eye instantly focused on me in the most accusing manner.

No worries? You just had to jinx us, didn't you?

Eleven

Leo's warning had come a little too late. The thing that gets me is that I did know better than to tempt fate, but I'd gone ahead and done it anyway. It wasn't that the spell had gone awry. Quite the contrary—I'd cast the divination perfectly.

Questionable.

No, my technique wasn't questionable. It was the results that had me baffled.

"Are you sure the man who murdered Kevin Paul wasn't George Mertes?" Heidi asked for the fifth time in the span of the past two minutes. She'd finished her wine and was twirling the empty glass by the stem. "I mean, you did say that the glare of the sun was in Mr. Paul's eyes when he was arguing with the killer. Seeing as you were witnessing everything he saw in his final moments, is it possible you couldn't get a good enough look at the murderer?"

Was the man's face warped? Like one of those Picasso paintings? Maybe you didn't add enough Kava Kava leaf. Ted is always shorting us on the Fijian plants.

"I added the exact same amount as the last time I'd cast this spell," I countered in frustration, staring at the empty pestles in front of me. I tossed my hands up in defeat. "And the glare of the sun wasn't enough to prevent me from seeing who Kevin Paul argued with right before he turned around and was hit on the head. For some reason, I could only see half the killer's face. Oh, I do recall that the killer had a massive combover. What was left was a bit greasy. I didn't recognize him, but it's not like we've met every single carnival worker that George Mertes has on staff."

"True," Heidi replied, casting a glance toward the kitchen. This setback did deserve a bit more wine. I stood and stretched my legs before making my way to the island where a half-bottle of wine was waiting to be finished. "Jack or Liam must have photographs of those they feel are part of the drug trafficking ring. Maybe we can come up with an excuse as to why you need to see them. You can always claim you suddenly recalled a man walking away from the kissing booth."

Leo was now sitting on the couch beside Heidi as we tried to figure out who the murderer could have been. It wasn't Elroy Simpson, because I'd seen the man's mugshot from a previous crime. He couldn't have changed all that much.

"What if the man doesn't work for the carnival at all?" I speculated, trying to think through the case the way Liam would if he'd been given this information. "What if the murderer was the supplier or maybe even a buyer of whatever drugs George and Olive are trafficking through the carnival? Could Kevin Paul have been in on the operation and tried to cut George out of the deal? Maybe this stranger I saw was working for the other side."

Look, Columbo. All these lovely theories are nothing but sheer conjecture. Let the good ol' sheriff and that oaf of a state police detective deal with these criminals. We took our best shot, we failed, and now we can enjoy the rest of our evening in the fashion which we've grown accustomed. Time for my evening pipe.

I disagreed with Leo. After all the effort we'd put into finding out who murdered Kevin Paul, it was going to be all for naught. I had a hard time accepting defeat, though.

Really? I find it relatively easy to let go, except when it comes to Skippy and his clan of ninja squirrels. I could be working on my next great plan to snatch the acorn from his paw, but your little escapades have been eating up my creative time. Can we please be done now?

It was highly doubtful that Liam would believe me if I suddenly had an epiphany that I'd seen the face of the murderer. I highly doubted that his unfailing belief in me stretched quite that far. A sketch artist would have come in handy right about now.

Then there was another problem—I hadn't been able to see the killer's shirt clearly. If it had been a grey set of overalls, thus indicating that he'd been a carnival worker, I'd be able to pick him out from the other employees on staff. Not knowing either way, this exercise could be like finding a needle in a haystack.

What if the murderer had already left town? Then I would never be able to find justice for the man whose body I'd stumbled over.

"It's only eight o'clock on a Saturday evening," my mother pointed out, standing from her seat in the overstuffed chair as if she were on a mission. She set her hands on her hips as if she'd come to a major decision. A wave of unease rolled over my stomach because my mother's plans usually had me doing something I didn't want to do. In this case, she might very well propose that I break my promise to Liam. "You swore to Liam that you'd stay away from the carnival tonight, but I did no such thing."

Your mother has never watched a horror flick, has she? I'm fairly sure we still have "The Texas Chainsaw Massacre" on DVD. There are definitely some lessons to be learned from that classic, not the first of which is not to marry your sister. Lesson number one—the first person who separates from the group is usually the first victim...or the killer. It really depends on the director. Hmmmm. Perhaps I've stumbled upon—

"Do you think I don't know about your annual conflict with Skippy and the other poor squirrels living in this small town?" my mother asked with that infamous arched eyebrow. Leo's whiskers twitched at the underlying threat she'd just given. "Now, where were we? Ah, yes! I'll give Beetle a call and see if he would like to join me for a funnel cake for two. I've had a hankering ever since I set foot in town, knowing I'd be here during the Spring Festival."

Raven, I don't know about you, but I'm getting numerous disturbing visions of the kind of trouble your mother can get Beetle into...and it's not very pretty. May I remind you how I get when I don't have my catnip? Beetle is my sole supplier of premium organic catnip in the county. He gives me edibles every morning. Should something happen to him, I cannot be held responsible for what actions I might take in response.

"You're getting on my very last nerve, Leo," my mother warned, crossing over to where her purse was located on the entry table beside mine. She reached into her bag and pulled out her cell phone, a little too eager to place a call to my part-time employee. "Oh, look at that! Beetle had the very same thought. He already texted me. Isn't that convenient?"

I'll admit to being a bit unnerved. Mother's sleight of hand was unmatched. The radiant smile that lit up my mother's pretty features was unlike any delight I've seen on her before. In the shop earlier this morning, I'd been pretty sure she'd put on an air about flirting with Beetle. She'd even admitted to it, but this? This woman standing before me? She was...happy.

It's a scary look on her, isn't it? A lot like Mad Cow disease.

Had I been closer to the couch, I would have knocked Leo on the head with the wine bottle. I found my mother's newfound joy rather refreshing. She'd grown more sarcastic over the years, and it didn't help that I'd all but thrown every-thing she'd tried to mold me into right out the window for the one thing she'd never wanted for me—life as a witch.

"Mom, I'm not so sure attending the carnival this evening is the right thing to do," I said cautiously, not wanting to be the one to wipe the smile from her face. "Liam wouldn't have asked us to stay home if he didn't believe that was the safest choice."

I can't believe I'm saying this, but I once again agree with the good ol' sheriff. We should all stay here, although your mother is free to go visit with Ted and mend the rift that has materialized between them. I'm sure that shed could hold the two of them quite comfortably. He has a space heater, right?

"Raven has a point, Mrs. M," Heidi said supportively, tucking her legs underneath her on the couch as she turned around to address my mom. "Jack texted me a bit ago, making sure that Raven and I were here at home. Whatever sting they are hoping to bring off tonight, it sounds pretty dangerous."

That means that Skippy and his fellow band of scoundrels will be hiding in the trees tonight. They're vulnerable to stray gunfire, you know. At least one good thing has come from this murder mystery, and that's keeping those squirrels from wreaking havoc and overrunning this town.

"It couldn't be that dangerous if Liam is allowing all the

other residents of Paramour Bay to attend the festivities this evening," my mother reasoned, her long red nails not getting in the way of her fingers rapidly flying over the display of her phone. Her smile somehow brightened even more with a sly twist. "Did you know that there are fireworks scheduled for ten o'clock?"

Do you think this is all Rosemary's doing? Maybe she found out about the time I tried to melt Ted with a match after he stepped on my tail. In my defense, having a six-and-a-half-foot giant stand on my tail might have caused me to experience temporary insanity.

"Mom, you're missing Liam's point." I did agree that he wouldn't have allowed the festivities to go on as planned if he thought being at the carnival would jeopardize anyone's life, but I wasn't just another pretty face. Having come to that conclusion produced a bright smile of my own. "I get that you enjoyed spending time with Beetle today, but we promised Liam we'd stay home tonight."

"You promised him, dear. Not me, nor Beetle." My mother finally stopped texting and dropped the phone into her purse as if that was the final word on the subject. A shot of fear went through me when my mother plucked my car keys from the wooden bowl I'd replaced after Leo had broken the previous porcelain one. "Seeing as you and Heidi are going to drink wine all evening, you won't be needing your car. I'll call you should I spot a man with a combover of greasy hair. What color did you say it was?"

Don't answer her, Raven! This is nothing more than a trap to get us to follow her, and we're not going to do it. We're standing our ground, right? Keeping our word to the good ol' sheriff?

"Blackish," I replied, quickly handing off the bottle of wine to Heidi as I continued toward the front door. "Mom, don't you dare do anything foolish. Stay in crowds, remain by Beetle's side, and call me immediately if anything out of the ordinary happens."

And just what do you think you'll do then, genius? Fly over to the carnival on the broom your mother obviously used to get here?

"Leo will be there in a flash to help should you need him." My response was mostly meant for my mother, but Leo got the gist. "And I'll call Liam to the rescue, if necessary."

I'm...flabbergasted. You just threw me under the bus, Raven. All six tires, including the back duals. I'm not even sure Skippy would have done such a thing. We share a code of honor. That really hurt, Raven.

"Stop being overly dramatic," I replied before turning back to face my mother. "I'm serious, Mom. Stay safe."

"You know very well I can defend myself against a mere human killer." My mother slung the strap of her purse over her shoulder as if I'd just insulted her. "Don't wait up for me. If plans go accordingly, I'll be quite late. Ta-ta!"

Thank the sweet angel of mercy, she's finally gone. Where's my pipe?

And just like that, my mother walked out the front door as if Paramour Bay didn't have a killer on the loose. The only sound was the slightest swish of pouring wine. My best friend knew me so well.

Me, too. I'll take a saucer.

Heidi didn't have to be a witch to know that Leo had all but demanded his catnip, his pipe, and a saucer of wine. Now that the rest of the evening was going to pass by very, very slowly.

"I should probably warn Liam." I slowly made my way back to the overstuffed chair my mother had vacated, sinking into the comfortable cushion after I'd snagged my wine glass from Heidi. I did have to grimace when I saw that Heidi had poured Leo's catnip in a small mound on the coffee table. Leo was already rolling on top of the minty herb, quickly spreading the green, tasty bits all over the surface. It would no doubt get stuck in the hand-carved crevices and drive him crazy for months. "It's too bad I can't give him a description of the killer."

"What if you could?" Heidi had a hint of glimmer in her blue eyes. That alone told me she'd come up with one of her wild and crazy plans. "What if I figured out a way for you to give Liam and Jack the information without them suspecting a thing?"

Leo had stopped wiggling and lay perfectly still on the coffee table, staring up at the ceiling without blinking.

I couldn't have just one night of peace, now could I?

"I'm game," I replied with enthusiasm, taking a fortifying sip of my wine. Was it so wrong to want to take a ride on the Ferris wheel with Liam so that we could sneak that notorious kiss at the top? "What do you have in mind?"

Twelve

I'm having déjà vu again...this is like the hundredth time in the past six months I've known about something before it happened. That's a low estimate, by the way. Have I mentioned recently that this is a bad idea?

Leo didn't have to convey his mantra concerning the past six months, because I was in full agreement. Heidi's plans were usually chock full of really, really bad ideas.

"I can't do it."

Has the supernatural realm frozen over? Are you actually taking my advice?

"Raven, it's the only way you can make sure that Liam has a description of the killer. How else are Liam and Jack going to make an arrest?"

"The old-fashioned way. Hard and persistent work following up leads."

We need to mark this date on a calendar. It could replace my birthday as the best day ever. So this is what pride in my accomplishments feels like. I should get some kind of ribbon or maybe even a trophy. It's not as effective as a bag of catnip, but it's a close second. That would be good. I might actually be on a roll here. Skippy better batten the hatches, because I'm gunning for him the next time he starts chucking acorns.

"Heidi, I've done nothing but lie to Liam about who and what I am," I explained, holding the cell phone tightly in my hand after I couldn't make the call she'd suggested. "I've done my best to be truthful about everything else in my life. My family's legacy is the only thing I've left out, but it's a major part of my life that I can't share with the man I'm falling in love with. Do you know how that feels? How it tears me apart? I actually thought of your plan myself earlier today, but I can't do it. I can't."

That's my girl. I'll just hop on the net and order that trophy we talked about. What's your PayPal password again?

Heidi and I had been talking about her plan for the last hour, going over the pros and cons. She'd suggested that I call Liam and tell him that I saw someone standing outside my cottage, thereby giving him the exact description of the killer. Yes, it was a way to communicate important details of the murder without disclosing how I'd come by the information, but I'd be telling another lie. It would be just one more knife in the back, and it would just make me feel worse about myself than I already did.

Eh, you get used to the weight of it all after a while. Not that I want you to change your outlook on this particular subject.

"Liam and Jack are conducting the drug sting tonight. It's not right to distract him, causing him to go on a wild goose chase looking for some intruder I made up, pulling his concentration off what could be a very dangerous assignment." I set down my cell phone and leaned forward enough to reach into one of the secret drawers of the coffee table that held my family's grimoire. "Leo, do you know if there's a spell where I can project a thought into someone else? Like when Mother caused Heidi to call me that one time, because she thought something might be wrong?"

There's a spell for practically everything, but isn't that the same as lying? You're going to have to be clearer with your intentions, because I'm not seeing the difference between what you're suggesting and what Heidi asked you to do, with the exception of the method of notification. Raven, don't make this euphoric feeling disappear. Do the right thing here.

"You're right," I conceded, sharing with Heidi the reason Leo was concerned. "I'd also be messing with Liam's thoughts, and I can't bring myself to cast a spell on him. We've found ourselves in quite the pickle, haven't we?"

I hate pickles. Not nearly as much as my aversion to a Connecticut genus fox squirrel named Skippy, but I'd say pickles are at the bottom of my list of adversaries.

"You needed an object that was owned by Kevin Paul to see his last thoughts, right?" Heidi pointed out, clearly having another idea form in that brilliant head of hers. "Jack didn't mention to me what was used to hit Mr. Paul on the back of the head, but did you see anything in the combover guy's hand that suggested what could have been used as the murder weapon? Maybe it's still at the scene of the crime."

Heidi dearest is a little too smart for her own good. I do appreciate brilliance in every form, but hers is liable to land us both in a boiling cauldron of witch hazel oil I have reserved for Skippy.

"No, I couldn't make out anything like that. I saw Kevin Paul's last few seconds, and he had his back to the killer when he was struck from behind." I did like the fact that Heidi was thinking outside the box and with magic. Witchcraft was my sole weapon, and I needed to use my supernatural abilities to my advantage. "What did Bulldog look like?"

"At least three or four inches over six feet, a buzz cut, and biceps larger than my thighs."

This Bulldog sounds like a potential special forces recruit I could use for my anti-rodent army I'm forming to deal with the likes of Skippy.

"What about Seymour?"

Heidi's eyebrow rose with a tilt of her head. She even pursed her lips as if we might have hit the nail on the head.

You'd have to be swinging the hammer right, and we all know that your natural sense of aim is off by a mile.

"I don't recall seeing Seymour. Leo did say that Olive and George were talking about hiding evidence, and she was the one to bring up Seymour's name," Heidi pointed out, excitement getting the both of us. "Maybe we can call your mother and have her seek him out to see if he has a combover."

My cell phone vibrated on the coffee table. Heidi and I exchanged quick glances, figuring it was my mother calling to tell us she'd located a carnival worker with a greasy combover. Only it was Liam's name that showed on the display.

The good ol' sheriff does have excellent timing.

"Hi," I replied softly after I'd accepted the call. It was easy to tell that he was at the carnival. Shouts, laughter, and all the familiar rings of the different rides could be heard in the background. I raised my voice a bit louder so that I would be easier to hear. "Is everything okay?"

"Better than okay. How does a ride on the Ferris wheel sound?"

By this time, Heidi had scooted to the end of the couch and was leaning forward in an attempt to find out why Liam was calling. Leo was still splayed out across the coffee table, his entire focus on me.

"A ride on the Ferris wheel?" I reiterated so that Heidi and Leo could follow along with the conversation. "Does that mean everything went okay with the sting?"

"Jack and his men did a fantastic job rounding up those involved in the drug ring," Liam prided, giving credit where credit was due. "Three arrests were made, one was taken in for questioning concerning another lead, and Jack is escorting them to the county jail to be processed through the system as we speak. Jack wanted me to tell Heidi that he'll be in touch after he's finished the initial paperwork tonight."

There were so many questions I wanted to ask, but the wrong one would clue Liam in that I knew more about the case than I should. I technically shouldn't know George Mertes, Olive, or Clara. I wasn't even sure Clara was one of the people involved, but I could safely assume that George and Olive were part of the four in custody.

Although if George Mertes had been arrested, why was the carnival still operating? Was there an alternate individual in the management chain when it came to the traveling business? I wasn't quite sure how carnivals worked nowadays.

You had to have been a reporter in your past life. Questions, questions, and more questions. Let it go, Raven. Like the song says...let it go.

"I'll relay the message to Heidi." I slowly closed the family grimoire and set it on the coffee table beside Leo. It appeared that there was no need for me to cast another spell, yet the palm of my hand still held that tingling sensation that forewarned me that not all the danger had passed. "Were the three individuals arrested all part of Kevin Paul's murder? That poor man."

That was a legitimate question, right?

It's still a question, Raven. Still another question.

Leo had been hanging out with Beetle too long. He was beginning to repeat phrases too many times for my liking, but I ignored his new annoying habit to concentrate on Liam's answer.

"Jack is confident that Kevin Paul's murder is related to the drug trafficking, but we'll know more once he's able to question the three individuals in custody. They all layered up, so it's going to take time to get the answers we need and maybe some deals to be made. With that said, I'm sure one of them will want to try to sell out their fellow drug dealers for a lesser sentence. Enough shop talk, Miss Marigold. How about that ride on the Ferris wheel? It's still early, the carnival is in full swing, and I actually have it on good authority that we can have the best seat overlooking Paramour Bay. That is, if I tip the ride operator."

It was hard to resist an offer like that, yet there was a slight problem with that plan. Actually, two. Well, three, but I was really trying hard to find a way to make sure that I could enjoy the rest of tonight without feeling as though an energy bolt was going to escape my hand at the slightest twitch.

Speaking of twitches, I've got mental whiplash over here. I can think of ten to twenty problems with your whacked-out plan, but most of my issues all include keeping the fact that you're a witch from the good ol' sheriff. I'm betting your list of problems doesn't include any of mine, am I right?

"Mom borrowed my vehicle to meet up with Beetle," I said, setting the main problem on the plate first.

You just had to remind me.

"I'm sorry," Liam said, a hint of laughter to his rich voice. I'm sure everyone would feel the same way once they saw my mother walking around the carnival with Beetle. With my luck, he'd even win her one of those oversized teddy bears. "I thought I heard you say that your mother was attending the carnival with Beetle."

"I did," I laughed, thankful that the murder mystery was wrapping up and that we could go back to enjoying our lives. If only the palm of my right hand agreed. "And that means I have no ride."

Heidi always took the train into town from New York City, so she didn't have a vehicle, either. We could technically walk, but it would take a while to get to the other end of town.

You want to walk into town on a road that is lined with nut-bearing trees, allowing Skippy and all of his minions to carry out their attacks at will? I don't think so.

"I'll swing by and pick you up. Ask Heidi to join us, but just make sure she knows I want you all to myself on that Ferris wheel ride."

Liam and I had been growing closer and closer since the beginning of the year, and I can honestly say that no man has ever made me feel as if I were the only woman in the world. He had the ability to do it with just a glance, but there were times like now that his rich voice dropped another octave and sent goosebumps chasing one another across my sensitive skin.

"That sounds perfect," I replied softly, ready to spend some quality time with Liam. Life had been a bit crazy lately, and it would be nice to slow it down a bit. "We'll be waiting for you and your chariot to arrive."

I feel a hairball stuck at the back of my throat.

"Jack and Liam made several arrests, the sting was successful, you have a message for me, and we're going to the carnival," Heidi summed up rather succinctly, not moving from the couch as she waited for me to convey Jack's message. "Why do I get the feeling I'm about to play the role of third wheel tonight?"

Tell my sweet Heidi that she can stay home and keep me company.

"You're not going to be a third wheel," I protested, not sure Heidi was going to like being a lone wheel, either. "But you can use this opportunity to seek out Seymour to see what he looks like. Apparently, the drug sting went according to plan, but not one word was said about Kevin Paul's murder. Jack wanted you to know that he'll touch base with you after he's through processing the paperwork."

Jack. Who names their son Jack, anyway? Sure, he was nimble and quick, but what person in their right mind jumps over an open flame?

"Who was arrested tonight?" Heidi asked, stretching as she stood. Her cute slip-on shoes were over near the door, as were the knee-high boots that I could still get away with in this spring weather. I had no doubt that the night was a bit chilly, but nothing a knitted sweater couldn't fix. "George?"

"I didn't want to ask too many questions up front," I fessed up, following Heidi over to the door. I removed my fuzzy slippers and began to put on my black knee-high boots. "Liam said that there were three arrests, so I'm assuming George and Olive. As for the third, maybe Clara? It's possible that her involvement was what led Kevin Paul to do the same, resulting in his death. Unfortunately, that means whoever killed Mr. Paul is still free to kill again."

Which is why I'm suggesting that we all stay in until the carnival leaves town. That would be safer for everyone involved. Sometimes I think I'm the only one in this house who has any common sense. Hey, I have a question. Is it possible to be in love with an inanimate object?

Leo's question gave me pause. For a brief moment, I thought he was referring to Ted and the golem's affection for the mannequin in Mindy's boutique. Awareness dawned when I witnessed Leo rubbing his back all over the coffee table. He must be trying to reach those small fragments of catnip that had fallen into the grooves of the hand-carved wooden surface.

"When Jack said three arrests, was he only talking about those who work at the carnival? What about who they were selling to or buying from? There had to be more people involved." Heidi reached into her purse, pulling out a hair tie. She was ready to get serious in her hunt for a man with a greasy combover. "There's a good chance the man who murdered Kevin Paul is already in custody."

Exactly. Now we can all have fun. I won't wait up for you two.

"Well, I can't think of a solid reason why we would ask Liam to see their mug shots." I finished zipping up my right boot, having already done so with my left. I shook out my skirt to make sure that the fabric looked as good as it did when I'd gotten dressed this morning. The only thing left to do was freshen up, because I already answered my own question. "Heidi, I have the perfect rationale as to why I'd want to see who was arrested. I could simply say that maybe I would recognize someone from the night I tripped over Kevin Paul's legs. Right? I mean, it makes perfect sense."

Nothing you say ever makes sense. It's alright to be defective, you know, as long as you take the first step and admit it to yourself.

"It does make sense, Leo. You've just consumed too much catnip to make any rational judgments."

I was feeling more like myself now that we had a solid plan in place. Liam should be able to pull up some photographs on the computer in his truck, I'd be able to make an identification, and then we could ride to the top of the Ferris wheel just like the happy couple always managed to do in the movies. The evening could end on the perfect note.

Have we not discussed the dangers of dangling a carrot in front of fate? You might be feeling more like yourself, but I have a feeling that my quiet night at home with my catnip and pipe just went up in smoke.

Thirteen

"...was involved," Heidi said chattily, having been discussing the drug sting since we'd gotten into Liam's truck. It was the kind of F150 with a cab that had a backseat, and I had no doubt that Leo was back there with her. "It sounds like everything went smoothly in the end. I just wish whoever murdered that poor man would be willing to confess and give some measure of closure to Mr. Paul's family."

"Jack is working on that as we speak," Liam said, braking slightly when the headlights of his truck glared off a small animal in the brush alongside the road. "The three suspects who are in custody have all lawyered up, but I'm sure some minor plea deals will be offered in exchange for information once the prosecutor comes on board."

Was it Skippy who was hiding in the brush alongside the road or one of his minions? I told you that furry rat has been monitoring my movements.

Leo was definitely in the backseat with Heidi, but I could tell by his breathless tone that he was working his way to the front, where he could be close to the windshield.

"Do you think that Kevin Paul was murdered because of the drugs that were being trafficked through the carnival?" I asked, peering over at Liam as he concentrated on the road. We were already a few streets away from where we would turn on the road to the carnival. "What if it was personal? Buttons did mention that Mr. Paul was dating one of the other carnival workers named Clara. Do you think it's possible that something went wrong in their relationship?"

The good ol' sheriff already said that things are taken care of, so could you leave well enough alone? It's Skippy we have to worry about. It's a conspiracy to eliminate feline familiars. I'm pretty sure those were his beady little eyes staring out at us from the side of the road.

"Anything is possible," Liam said somewhat cautiously, releasing his hold of the steering wheel with his right hand to reach out for mine. His warmth enveloped me as we interlaced our fingers on top of a manila folder. "Don't worry. Jack will keep me updated on anything that develops."

I noticed that Liam didn't say whether or not Clara was part of the three suspects currently in custody. He really did play his cards close to his chest. His level of caution made me worry that he might not trust me completely. It wasn't like I had a right to be upset.

Skippy is the same way. Always with the open-ended options. I feel your pain.

"Enough about all that craziness," Liam advocated with a light squeeze, flipping on the turn signal as we came to the intersection of River Bay and Oceanview Drive. "I wasn't sure we'd get to enjoy the Spring Festival, but Jack has assigned a couple of his state patrol officers to keep their eyes on the carnival until Monday morning. With everything that took place, he didn't want to miss anything should there be some loose threads that need to be dealt with."

I'd normally give the detective credit, but I won't. He's not good enough for my Heidi, no matter how hard he tries.

Basically, Jack had lightened Liam's responsibility with the added security. Yes, the carnival did employ a couple of security guards, but once the enterprise was compromised, none of their people could be trusted. Not to mention that the state police were armed. They also had considerably more training, and their loyalties weren't in question.

"Does that mean you are off duty for the rest of the night?" I asked, still trying to figure out a way to bring up the description of the man I saw during the spell I'd cast earlier this evening. The struggle was real. I shouldn't have to lie to the man I was dating, and I could feel myself reaching the end of that rope. "I'm beginning to see a funnel cake in our future."

Don't worry. I have an endless stash of rope to keep feeding you. Remember, the council agreed to let the whole Heidi thing slide. Let's not push them into taking action by having half the town of Paramour Bay realize that the supernatural realm really does exist.

Two people certainly didn't make up the entire town, but I did receive Leo's message loud and clear.

"With an extra sprinkle of powdered sugar, right?" Liam said, expertly maneuvering the truck into the spot he'd reserved for his emergency vehicle near the carnival. Two state police cruisers were parked nearby, bracketing the entrance to the park. He released my hand so that he could shift into park. "I did tell Jack that I'd check in with the officers he'd left behind to patrol the carnival grounds a couple of times until close. Other than that, we'll see if I can't win you a stuffed animal from one of the shooting games. I'm pretty sure it's rigged, but

I figured out the count of the metal targets by watching a few of the kids throwing their dollars away this afternoon."

If the good ol' sheriff gives me a couple of hours, I can have a few squirrels tied to those metal targets. Nothing like a little realism to stir the pot.

Had we been anywhere else, I would have given Leo a tap on the head. He talked a good game, but he'd never really go through with hurting a squirrel.

You keep telling yourself that, missy. You'll end up waking up with Skippy in your bed. He's pushed me to the edge of that proverbial rope you were talking about, and my entire stash is dedicated to you.

"I was thinking of visiting Bulldog for that relish recipe, so why don't I catch up with you two in, say…maybe an hour?" Heidi suggested, tapping the purse she'd brought with her. It was one of those small crossbody purses that she could keep close without fearing someone would steal it. "I think we got our signals crossed earlier today."

"You mean when you and Raven took a stroll over to the trailers snooping around for Scott Larson's camper?" Liam had commented in such a nonchalant manner that I almost missed the fact that he'd known all along we'd been caught red-handed. My attention was also on the fact that the manila folder that had been underneath our hands actually had something to do with the drug sting that had just taken place. "For your information, Scott "Bulldog" Larson was instrumental with the success of the arrests this evening. Let's just say he might have mentioned that the two of you had a bit more interest in Kevin Paul's murder than the average local citizen."

You guys are so busted.

I fully expected Heidi to launch into one of her cover

stories, but her silence spoke volumes. This was completely on me, and I wasn't going to lie anymore.

Wait. What? Raven, don't you dare—

"It's true that Heidi and Bulldog had talked about relish recipes, but we had also run into Buttons. He'd told us all about the woman Kevin Paul was dating, and we decided to go talk to her. It was foolish in retrospect, but at the time it seemed like a good idea," I said, keeping as close to the truth as I could. No more lies, despite Leo's stress level rising to the point that he was choking up another hairball. Bottom line? Liam deserved better. "Liam, we were never in danger. We were just talking to the carnival workers, hoping that we would uncover something that could help your investigation."

I never thought I'd go out by a hairball. I guess death can happen in the strangest ways. I mean, I've accepted that you'll be the reason for my demise, but a hairball? Being taken out by Skippy would be a more honorable death. Where is that ninja and his acorns when you need him?

Liam had removed the keys from the ignition without really acknowledging what I'd said, causing a sliver of unease to slice through my heart. He got like this sometimes, and it was always when I stretched the truth about a situation regarding witchcraft. Let's face it—magic and spells were a big part of who I'd become in these last six months.

Do I need to go find your mother? She's not the most ideal person to bail you out of this situation, but at least she'd prevent you from doing something you'll regret. Worst case, I'll go to Skippy. I'm sure he and his band of merry rats can cause enough of a distraction to keep the good ol' sheriff busy while we make a clean getaway.

"How about you leave the policework to me and Jack from now on?" Liam tossed a grin my way, which I caught due to the streetlight above. I could still sense that he knew there was something more to the picture than I'd painted, but it seemed that he wasn't going to let it ruin the rest of the night. "I'd rather not go grey in my thirties."

See? Nothing to worry about. He doesn't suspect a thing. Not that I believed you'd bring our world crashing down around us. Not for a second.

Liam opened his door and stepped out onto the sidewalk. He closed the door with a wink, but his lighter outlook didn't make me feel any better. It didn't escape me that he hadn't even asked why we'd do such a thing as to get involved with someone's murder investigation.

"He knows something isn't right," I whispered, trying not to move my lips as Liam came around the front of the truck to open our doors. To find someone so kind, compassionate, and loyal was so hard in this life. If I wasn't careful, I'd lose him and the promise of a healthy and wholesome relationship. "What am I going to do?"

Didn't we just cover this?

"You're going to enjoy this evening and worry about it later."

Heidi gives such good advice, doesn't she? I just love that woman.

I hadn't brought a purse like Heidi, but I had brought my cell phone, along with my identification and some money tucked in the back of the case. It had slipped a bit when Liam had held my hand, but I easily found it in the crevice of the seat. In doing so, the manila folder shifted and the corner of a sheet of pictures had glided out. The white glare of the artificial light beaming down from the street lamp made it hard to see anything else but the faces of three men.

A zap of energy hit my palm out of nowhere.

Don't say it.

"Heidi, I—"

The passenger side door opened before I could finish my stunning announcement. Liam held out his hand, and I had no choice but to take his kind gesture. I dropped my cell phone back in my seat with every intention of reaching back inside the cab of the truck. My plan worked brilliantly.

Your definition of that word continues to baffle me completely. One of these days, we'll have to sync up our internal dictionaries. Of course, that might totally destroy my understanding of the English language.

The line of photographs, six of them in total on the one sheet, didn't contain any names...only random numbers beneath their picture. The man in the top corner was the individual I saw when I'd cast the spell earlier this evening. The case was solved...but only if I could somehow relate that to Liam without revealing my supernatural secret.

Fourteen

You're looking at this wrong, Raven. If the man who killed Kevin Paul is in that group of pictures, doesn't it stand to reason that the man is now in custody? One of the others will most certainly cut a deal to reduce his or her sentence by turning state's evidence on Mr. Greasy Combover.

Yes, but Jack and Liam didn't technically know that for certain. Maybe, just maybe, the man would confess after being questioned by Jack. Apparently, the murderer had worked at the carnival all along. Granted, many people were required to be employed by a carnival in order to keep it functioning on such a high level. I hadn't met every single employee or even seen them all, so it only made sense that I hadn't run into the man before now.

Our job was done when we determined Rye wasn't involved, and our reputation in the afterlife remains intact. The sheriff captured the non-supernatural killer. Let him finish up the job on his own.

"Did you see the new caramel apples they have for sale?" Liam asked, resting his hand on my lower back as we continued to walk through the throngs of people enjoying their brisk spring evening. The carnival was in full swing, and everyone seemed to be having a great time playing games and riding the various stomach-churning rides. "Instead of an apple on a stick, the apple is cut up into wedges in a Styrofoam bowl with warm caramel sauce drizzled over the smaller slices. We'll have to try some after we're done riding the Ferris wheel. First up on our agenda is that funnel cake you've talked about all week."

Raven, our part of the case is solved. The bad guy is behind bars. Can you go stuff your face in peace while I see what Skippy is up to? He's been awfully quiet today. Too quiet, if you know what I mean. He must be preparing for a surprise attack.

There was no reason that I shouldn't enjoy this night with Liam, with the exception that the tingling sensation in the palm of my right hand had yet to subside. Was it because a confession hadn't been obtained yet?

Yes. Does that answer your question? I'm off to confront my time-honored nemesis. I know this is a rather big favor to ask, but please don't get into any trouble while I'm gone.

"How about that stuffed animal you promised me?" I all but dared Liam with a little shoulder bump, taking Leo's advice. There were a million reasons why the energy around me hadn't settled, one of them being my mother gallivanting around the carnival with Beetle in tow. We hadn't run into them yet, but I'm sure it was just a matter of time. "Isn't that the shooting game you were boasting about?"

"No pressure, right?" Liam asked with a laugh, seemingly forgetting all about what had been said in the truck. Heidi had immediately veered off when we'd walked through the entrance of the carnival, allowing me and Liam to enjoy some time alone. "What are we aiming for? The unicorn, the teddy bear, or the lion?"

148

"The classic teddy bear, of course. He can even ride the Ferris wheel with us." Even though the annoying pricks and piercing pain dancing inside my palm remained unabated, I could feel the tension leaving my shoulders as we walked up to the game booth. "I call middle seat, though."

"I wouldn't have it any other way," Liam replied, stealing a kiss before reaching into the back pocket of his jeans for his wallet. He looked up at the woman who was running the game. "What's the damage going to be?"

"Three dollars, sir," the redhead said with a smile. She had a sprinkling of freckles over the bridge of her red-tinted nose and cheeks, reminding me of that cowgirl in *Toy Story*. "If you can knock down one metal target, you can have your choice of the small stuffed animals. If you can take out two, you can choose from the medium-sized inventory. If you manage to strike all three, you'll win the mega-sized stuffed animal of your choice."

Liam rolled his shoulders after handing over a five-dollar bill. He began rolling up the sleeves to his black dress shirt. He must have headed home to change after the drug sting and the resulting arrests, and I was very appreciative as I inhaled deeply to capture the intoxicating scent of his aftershave. He wasn't one to overdo it with his cologne, either. Truthfully, it was just the right amount on both counts.

"You mean business," I laughed, realizing that I'd never been a recipient of a stuffed animal before. "I'm going to name my teddy bear Ferris, so don't let me down."

"Never." Liam flashed me another smile before picking up the undersized toy pellet gun. It looked so tiny in his hands, but he still settled the butt of the weapon against his shoulder as if it were the most natural thing in the world to him. He leaned down on the wooden counter to steady his aim. I almost took a step back to enjoy the view, but I didn't want to be too obvious. He certainly knew how to wear a pair of denim jeans. "Let's win you that bear."

By this time, some of the local children who knew Liam to be the sheriff had come over to see just how good he was at hitting the target. One boy's eyes had widened to the point that he reminded me of Leo.

"Not to put any more pressure on you, but Dee Fairuza's nephew is standing off to the side with idolization written all over his face," I whispered, leaning down so that only Liam could hear me. His chuckle told me that he knew exactly who was watching in our immediate area. "No pressure, though."

Liam's shoulders had been lifting in laughter, but he finally settled as he evened out his breathing. I realized he was doing that counting thing he'd mentioned before, and after thirty to forty seconds had passed, Liam ever so slowly squeezed the trigger.

Tink!

A round of cheers erupted from the boys and girls, whose group had grown exponentially. I had to admit that my heart swelled at the thought of carrying around an oversized teddy bear that had been won by someone so special.

Tink!

Another wave of encouragement had me just as excited, and I held my breath in anticipation for the third shot. True to Liam's word, he must have been counting those seconds he'd timed before ever handing over his money. Twenty seconds had passed this time, and the small pellet was finally discharged from the barrel...hitting the metal target directly in the middle and knocking it down.

Tink!

It was impossible not to jump up and down with the group of children who'd gathered around to watch, all of us clapping and laughing when the carnival worker handed me the over-sized teddy bear that I'd pointed to mid-leap the moment Liam had succeeded in knocking down all three targets.

"Liam, that was amazing!" I gushed, squeezing the light brown teddy bear whose head was five times the size of mine. "I'm pretty sure your performance was the final nudge Dee's nephew needed to confirm his future career."

Liam was modest as he brushed away the compliment, turning the conversation back to funnel cakes as if he hadn't been the first person to win the big prize at that particular game booth all weekend. Granted, the festivities had closed early last night, but it was still a huge accomplishment.

"Extra sugar?" Liam asked, getting in line with five other tourists and locals who'd had the same craving for funnel cakes as we had tonight. Who am I kidding? I'd been hankering for them since yesterday. "Why don't you grab us a picnic table? Ferris can share your seat."

I lugged the teddy bear over to a table that a family had just vacated, setting Ferris down and propping him up at the table with his oversized arms. I then sat on the end of the bench seat and looked around, having always enjoyed people watching.

"...hear about George? I knew something fishy was going on, but drugs?"

I barely caught the conversation between two of the workers behind me at the popcorn stand. A young girl was the cashier, while a middle-aged woman was serving tubs of the buttery snack. They'd stopped gossiping to serve a group of people.

The palm of my hand began to swell with a smidge more energy. Nothing seemed amiss around me, so the conversation behind me had to be the reason for my added unease. A squeal of delight pulled my focus, and I was greeted by the sight of

Buttons making a toddler screech with delight when a yellow balloon quickly turned into a giraffe.

By this time, Liam had managed to move up to the second position in line at the funnel cake stand.

I scanned the area carefully, wondering if my mother or Beetle was somewhere in the crowd. There was no sign of them, but I did catch a glimpse of Clara. She was manning the balloon game, even though I could see her eyes were still bloodshot from crying all day. Truthfully, I was surprised she was even working. Then again, the carnival had to be short-staffed with George, Olive, and the man responsible for murdering Kevin Paul currently in custody.

"...think George had something to do with Kevin's murder?"

"I don't know. I did find it odd that George fired Elroy like that, out of the blue."

"Kevin had nothing to do with that, though. It was..."

I'd been so caught up in the conversation behind me that I startled when Liam suddenly materialized before me with a funnel cake in hand. True to his word, there was extra powdered sugar on top.

"Are you okay?" Liam asked, a half grin on his face when he saw that I'd placed my hand over my heart. He lifted a denim-clad leg over the bench seat across from me, setting the paper plate down between us with a pile of napkins. "This should make up for me startling you while you were stargazing."

"What this is going to do is add a pound to my hips," I teased, trying to shake off the apprehension that I'd missed something important in the exchange between the two women at the popcorn stand. Liam had already torn off a small piece of funnel cake and held it up for me to take the first bite. I leaned forward and ended up closing my eyes as the sweet white sugar literally melted on my tongue. "Hmmmm. Oh, that's good. That's really good and totally worth the extra mile on the treadmill."

I'd lifted my lashes to find that Liam's brown eyes had darkened with desire. He silently reached forward and brushed my bottom lip with his thumb. Heat immediately spread over my body in a way that had nothing to do with Mother Nature or the supernatural. I'd been falling for this man ever since he'd come into the tea shop after I'd dialed 911. I'm pretty sure this was the beautiful moment I would look back on and realize that he was the one.

"Your hips are perfect just the way they are, Raven. I'm glad we got to spend some time together tonight," Liam said softly, leaning back ever so slightly so that he could also taste the funnel cake without disrupting our moment. "Otis and Karen invited me over to dinner next weekend. Would you like to join us?"

"I'd like that very much," I replied, knowing how important Otis and Karen were to Liam. The former sheriff and his wife had taken in Liam and his sister when they were in their teens. "Please let me know what I can bring. Maybe a dessert? I don't think I can make a funnel cake this good, but I do make a great pineapple upside-down cake with cherries to boot."

Liam and I spent the next five minutes in deep conversation about everything and anything that popped into our heads. I'd been swept up in the intimacy we'd created at our picnic table, and it was as if everyone else had dropped off the face of the planet. I hadn't even given a second thought to the two women in the popcorn booth until one of them walked by, probably to take her break.

"Something wrong?" Liam asked, glancing over his

shoulder in concern at where my gaze had followed the younger woman.

There were those times in life when a person was given a choice to make. I was presented with one now. I'm not talking about revealing my life as a witch, but I could definitely be more truthful and honest with the man who I wanted to take our relationship to the next level with in the very near future.

"I overheard that young girl talking with the other woman working the popcorn stand," I revealed without hesitation as I wiped my fingers on one of the napkins. "They said that Kevin wasn't responsible for getting Elroy Simpson fired."

Wow, it felt amazing to share what I'd found out about the case with Liam. Maybe he'd be able to call Jack so that he could use that bit of information in his interrogation.

"Really?" Liam grabbed a napkin, as well. He regarded the popcorn stand carefully before making a decision. "One of the men arrested tonight, Seymour Lincoln, made it sound as if Kevin had orchestrated the entire scenario of obtaining a job here at the carnival. Could you give me a minute? I'd like to ask the young lady a couple of questions."

It was good to know that Seymour had been the third individual who'd been taken into custody. He was the one Heidi and I suspected of having a combover. Maybe my hand still had a slight warmth to it due to the loose ends that still needed to be cleared up. Liam stood from the picnic table, but he came around my side and leaned down to steal a kiss before making his way over to the popcorn stand.

"There you are!" Heidi exclaimed from out of nowhere, quickly taking Liam's place across from me. "I have some news you're not going to like. Where's Liam?"

The night had been going so well, too. Hopefully, she was referring to something my mother had done, like using magic to get the ring around the neck of a bottle to win a prize. I was in the process of updating Heidi on the fact that Seymour Lincoln had been arrested and that we had nothing more to worry about when something to the right of the picnic table caught our attention.

Come back here, Skippy! I know it was you who threw that acorn at me, and I'm not going to stand for any more of your underhanded abuse!

We saw a squirrel bouncing across the grass in between the funnel cake booth and the Dippin' Dots trailer, with Leo doing his best to keep up with him on those short stubby legs of his. His hind end was wiggling back and forth as fast as he could make it, his green eyes glued to the quickly escaping squirrel.

The next sequence of events could have been straight out of a Saturday morning cartoon. Skippy launched himself into the air, landing on top of a garbage can that had one of those oversized lids. Leo didn't quite make the jump, but his comical attempt and subsequent headlong crash into the side of the barrel had Skippy scampering off the lid and right onto Button's wig.

Ouch.

If you thought that things had already gone south, it was nothing compared to the fuzzy red wig being caught in Skippy's claws and somehow trailing behind him as he ran off into the dark beyond the reach of the artificial lights. He'd left Leo in his dust and Buttons without a wig.

I might have a concussion. Raven, is that you over there?

"Uh, Raven?"

"I know," I whispered, stunned to see the combover I'd seen after casting the spell a few hours earlier. "Buttons killed Kevin Paul."

Leo was walking a bit sideways toward us when he heard me utter my conclusion. He blinked twice before slowly adjusting his focus on Lyle Gafney, a.k.a. Buttons.

It's always the freaking clown. Always.

"Raven," Liam called out, his rich voice taking Button's focus off the squirrel that had stolen his wig. "I hate to do this, but I'm going to have to—"

Buttons slowly stood, somehow realizing that we were all staring at him...and it had nothing to do with his combover. Whatever the worker at the popcorn stand had said to Liam, it had obviously pointed him in Button's direction. As for Heidi and me, well, we already knew the truth.

Run for your lives!

Fifteen

Liam had ordered Heidi and me to stay put as he took off running after Buttons. It was rather difficult to think of the man as Lyle. We'd shared a meal with him, watched as he created animals out of balloons for children, and felt bad over the loss of his friend. He'd tricked all of us.

He's a clown, Raven. That alone should say it all. Not everyone was fooled.

"I should go after them," I whispered to Heidi, glancing around at everyone who'd witnessed Liam chasing off after Buttons. The two had disappeared around the back of the funnel cake stand in mere seconds. "I can…"

I wiggled my fingers to indicate witchcraft so that Heidi understood what I was saying. What if Buttons had some type of gun that didn't just shoot out a flag that said *BANG*? What if he knew of some hiding places where he could lie in wait and attack Liam when he wasn't expecting it?

Isn't this exactly what the good ol' sheriff is trained to do? Well, I doubt he was trained to deal with clowns. Those mentally disturbed individuals are a special breed. Nevertheless, what you should be focused on is the fact that I might have bent my last straight whisker helping Skippy uncover the killer. Skippy one, Leo zero. Until next time, you furry rat!

Heidi had quickly scooped Leo up into her arms, cradling him to her chest while she dug into the small purse that was strapped over the front of her. It wasn't an easy feat, considering he weighed at least thirty pounds, but she managed to find her cell phone.

Twenty-nine pounds, Raven. Twenty-nine. Premium organic catnip helps with weight issues, you know.

"I'll call Jack." Heidi sat back down at the picnic table with Leo in her lap. "He—"

"There is one of the officers now," I exclaimed, pointing over to where one of the uniformed men must have seen Liam take off after Buttons. "I still think that—"

"You'll do nothing of the sort," my mother muttered, sidling up against me as she grabbed hold of my arm so I couldn't move from my spot. Beetle was a few yards back, his blue gaze glued to the last place Liam and Buttons had been seen. Well, he could join the club. "Focus. Tell me what you feel."

A badly bent whisker.

My mother's directive had caught me off guard, but it was long enough for me to notice the gathering energy around us. I did a double-take and met her knowing stare.

Someone was using magic.

Now that's a novel idea. Raven, this whisker wasn't bent by using black magic. We can fix it when we get home. I'm sure there's a spell in the grimoire somewhere.

"My, oh my!" Beetle exclaimed, finally joining the rest of us at the picnic table. His white hair practically glowed underneath the artificial lights. "Did you see that? Why, Liam went after that clown without a second's hesitation. No hesitation whatsoever! What do you think that was all about?"

I've been thinking about my whisker. Maybe we should let your mother cast the spell. Let's face it, you still lack a certain finesse that she's already mastered.

With Beetle standing right in front of me, I contained my reaction to Leo's insult. It wasn't even so much the actual insult that dumbfounded me. It was the fact that there was only one other person who could have been using magic if my mother was standing by my side...and that was Rye.

Now you've garnered my attention. Why would our resident warlock be inserting himself into our investigation after he so adamantly refused to join our team?

"Beetle, would be a kind soul and go find me a glass of wine?" my mother asked with a few bats of her eyelashes. "The only booth with an alcohol permit is over by the Ferris wheel. Had I known we'd be enjoying a night out, I wouldn't have worn these gorgeous ankle boots."

She's as nauseating as Rowena, and that's saying quite a bit.

Mom raised her hand so fast that Leo practically scampered up Heidi's upper body, his mind no longer on his bent whisker.

"Anything for you, my dear Regina," Beetle crooned, giving a small bow before setting out to search for that red Solo cup of wine.

"Beetle, can you make that two?" Heidi called out, giving me an unapologetic shrug. She then stroked Leo in comfort, reassuring him that he hadn't turned into a toad. "Might as well join her, Raven."

Don't do it, Heidi. Don't join the dark side.

"This is really serious, Mom," I whispered now that Beetle was out of earshot. "Buttons was the one who killed Kevin

Paul. I saw a mugshot in a folder that Liam had in his truck, and I incorrectly assumed the man was named Seymour. George, Olive, and Seymour were arrested in that drug sting, but I have a feeling the ringleader was Buttons all this time."

"Look," my mother directed me with a tilt of her head toward where Liam had run off after Buttons. "You have nothing to worry about, and it seems that we've even made a friend in this mess."

I wasn't quite sure who my mother was talking about, but Liam suddenly emerged from the darkness, leading a hand-cuffed clown in the direction of the exit. Buttons' scowl was evident despite the smudged face paint, but it could easily have been the fact that he was now without a wig. He must have lost his red bulbous nose at some point, too, because that item was also missing.

If it hadn't been for the fact that I was seeking out the individual my mother could have been talking about, I would never have noticed Rye standing back in the shadows. His red and white plaid shirt was barely visible, but that's how I knew the man in question was my so-called cousin.

That was very smart of you, Rye. Listen, do you think we can have a one-on-one discussion about this abundant squirrel population in town? Your abilities could come in quite handy with my current Skippy situation.

Rye must have somehow aided Liam in apprehending Buttons, though I had to question if there might be strings attached to such an olive branch.

"Well, it looks as if another one of your murder mysteries has been solved," my mother commented as she stepped away from me. She even gave a small clap in celebration. "Try not to make a habit of getting involved with them. I'm on the downs-lope of life, and I'd really rather spend the rest of my years enjoying wine and the company of a very nice gentleman. Now, I'm off to enjoy the festivities with Beetle. Did you know that he can play the violin? Such a talented man. Ta-ta! Oh, and don't wait up for me."

My mother's laughter rang out behind her as she turned away.

Hairball.

I'd been so preoccupied watching my mother take her leave that by the time I looked back at the darkened area next to the funnel cake stand...Rye had completely disappeared.

"I've been texting Jack," Heidi divulged, setting her cell phone down on the table so that she could pay more attention to Leo. "He's on his way. Apparently, one of the officers had already notified him of what was taking place. He'll be here in around twenty minutes."

Grand. I don't like how Heidi ignores me when that man is around, Raven.

I had no choice but to take my seat next to the oversized teddy bear, but I did so in a way that I could still keep my eye on the path that Liam had taken with Buttons. There were so many questions that had been left unanswered, the main one being why Buttons had killed Kevin Paul.

You're missing the point, Raven. Even your mother pointed out that the murder mystery has been solved, so we can get back to setting a foolproof trap to capture Skippy. Is your palm still burning?

"No," I replied, only now realizing that the tingling sensation had slowly dissipated. "Buttons really did kill Kevin Paul."

"Oh, Raven," Heidi said softly, calling my attention to Clara. She was standing near the younger girl from the popcorn stand, who was trying to comfort the grieving girlfriend. "Clara must have realized that Buttons being arrested means that he was most likely involved in Kevin Paul's murder. That's so sad."

"At least Clara has some closure." I couldn't imagine what the poor woman was going through, but at least she had a good support group of friends around her. Around two or three other people in grey uniforms had joined her, one a man with very large biceps. "Is that Bulldog?"

"Yeah," Heidi said with an infectious smile. "That's what I was coming to tell you. I had a talk with Bulldog about his relish recipe and why he didn't rat me out. We already know that he was helping the police, but he mentioned how hurt he was by Seymour...and then showed me a picture. I was trying to find you before everything happened with Buttons to tell you that Seymour had jet black hair and a goatee—no combover. I guess we now know who does."

Leo had been using his front paw to try to fix his whisker, but he wasn't having any success. Heidi had decided that Beetle wasn't coming back with her wine, so she settled for the coffee I was able to get us from the funnel cake stand. We weren't sure how long Liam would be gone, and it was doubtful that Jack would have a moment to spare after he ended up taking Buttons into custody. Our best bet was to wait.

"Leo, I was thinking," I said, after at least another half an hour had gone by. We'd even enjoyed the small fireworks display that had taken all of five minutes, but Leo's disgruntled appearance was tugging at my heartstrings. "Skippy technically helped solve this case."

Leo's left eye might have protruded another millimeter in irritation, but he at least considered what I had to say about Skippy.

"Think about it. Had you not been chasing Skippy, he wouldn't have been running through the carnival. Therefore, he wouldn't have had the need to jump on top of that garbage can and land on Buttons' head," I rationalized, noticing that Leo had straightened up a bit while sitting on Heidi's lap. "Skippy somehow got a claw caught in Buttons' wig, and it was then we noticed his combover. Granted, Liam chased after Buttons for an entirely different reason based on whatever information he heard from the popcorn stand worker, but still...Skippy had a major role in the unveiling of a murderer."

He bent my whisker. That is totally unacceptable.

"Maybe you can cut Skippy a break, considering that Paramour Bay is now safe once again," I recommended, draining what was left of my coffee. The festivities of the carnival were winding down for the night, which told me that we might have to locate my mother for a ride home. "I'm sure we can fix your whisker, Leo."

"I think it adds character." Heidi was always good for Leo's ego. "Such a handsome kittycat. He's my boy."

I wonder how much it would take to bribe Skippy to run out in front of a certain state police detective's vehicle.

At least I had gotten Leo's mind off his whisker and the various ways he could get retribution. In the meantime, it was time to text my mother and hope that I wasn't interrupting anything that would result in ruining the rest of the weekend. Heidi and I still have a house to look at tomorrow morning. I'd just reached into my skirt pocket for my cell phone when I heard my name being called.

"Liam!" I exclaimed, quickly disengaging myself from the picnic table. "Are you okay?"

It was a silly question when I had seen for myself that he'd been physically fine after apprehending Buttons, but the question had popped out anyway.

"Yes. I'm just sorry it took so long for me to get back here.

Jack took Lyle Gafney into custody for the murder of Kevin Paul." Liam stroked his warm hands up and down my arms. My sweater prevented skin-on-skin contact, but the heat of touch still made its way through the thick fabric. "It's quite a story, if you and Heidi would like to hear it."

Wait. So, does that mean the oaf of a detective isn't joining Heidi tonight?

"Of course." I scooted the oversized teddy bear over on the bench seat so that we would both have room on the one side. Heidi and I were both anxious to hear what had really taken place for Buttons to take the chance of committing murder in broad daylight. "I can't believe that Buttons killed Kevin Paul. I mean, we had breakfast with him."

I'm sleeping next to Heidi tonight. We'll take the couch. You can have your mother.

"Jack was able to finally shed some light on the drug sting, which was connected to the murder," Liam shared, completely oblivious to Leo making tonight's sleeping arrangements. He straddled the bench seat so that he was facing me while being able to speak to Heidi as well. "George Mertes, the owner and operator of this traveling establishment, allowed Lyle Gafney, Olive Belvin, and Seymour Lincoln to run drugs through his operation in exchange for a ten percent of the action."

"That's horrible."

I would have asked for twenty.

"It gets worse," Liam warned, leaning an elbow against the table. "Elroy Simpson's body was recovered down in Alabama earlier this week. Turns out that Gafney murdered Simpson and forced George Mertes to hire Kevin Paul."

Another insider who wouldn't blow the whistle on the entire drug operation. You've got to admit...it was a genius plan.

"Why would Buttons—I mean, Lyle—kill Kevin Paul?" I

asked, not clear on why Buttons would kill one person only to end up killing his replacement.

Can you say, psychopath? He chose to be a clown, Raven. Who does that? And just so you know, even psychos can end up changing their minds. Wait a minute. Maybe that's why Skippy is always one step ahead of me. He's an unpredictable psycho ninja squirrel. Raven, we might just have a psychotic squirrel problem on our hands. See? I was right all along. He must have rabies!

"This is where we don't have the entire story, but we believe that Kevin Paul had a change of heart about the drug business once he began dating Clara. He wanted out, Gafney couldn't let him spill the beans, and one thing led to another."

"So, Kevin wanted to do the right thing?" Heidi asked, sadness lacing her soft tone as she continued to scratch Leo behind the ear. "Sometimes our poor choices get us in over our heads, and the only thing left to do is try to swim for shore."

"Or get eaten by the sharks," Liam summed up with a disappointed shake of his head. I tried not to take his analogy too seriously, because we weren't talking about my choices at the moment. "It's a shame that this year's Spring Festival was tarnished by all these arrests, but we were able to rid the streets of some very bad people."

Your choice to keep our lineage safe is for the best. You seem to be forgetting a very important tidbit. It's not just your secret, Raven. Others could be hurt by you revealing our abilities to humans...Heidi being the exception, of course. Besides, you're the one who brought up my weight. Look at me like your life preserver in stormy seas.

As I've often said, Leo never ceased to amaze me with his inopportune insight into certain situations. I wanted to steal him from Heidi and give him the biggest hug, but Liam might think that was a bit odd.

No public displays of affection, please. I have a reputation to uphold. Skippy might see.

"How about that Ferris wheel ride before we head home?" I asked Liam, reaching for his hand and squeezing his fingers in anticipation. "We deserve a little fun after all the work you did to keep this festival safe for the locals and tourists."

"We have around ten minutes before they shut this place down for the night." Liam had lifted his left arm to look at the time. "Heidi, would you watch the monstrosity I won for Raven? We won't be long, and I don't want to share my seat with anyone or anything but this beautiful woman here."

"Leo and I will follow behind," Heidi said, setting Leo on the ground and reaching over the table for Ferris. He was almost as big as her, but she managed to get an arm around his neck and lug him toward the Ferris wheel. "That way you guys don't have to double back to find us."

"By the way, how did Leo manage to show up back here in town?" Liam asked me as he kept hold of my hand and began to weave through the waning crowd to reach the Ferris wheel.

I could only laugh, purposefully not answering as we hurried along. The delicious aroma of popcorn and funnel cakes still hung in the air. We ran past the strings of lights and game booths as we raced against the clock. I wasn't the least bit sad that the temperature had dropped a few degrees, because that only meant I got to sit closer to this amazing man. More importantly, I had no desire to swim with the sharks, and Leo had already offered himself up as a life preserver. He'd made a good point when he reminded me that the supernatural realm wasn't only my secret to keep.

My decision to keep quiet had nothing to do with lack of

trust or what Liam's possible reaction could be to such an unbelievable announcement. It had more to do with the fact that I wasn't the only supernatural being in existence, and I needed to take into consideration their lives, as well. Should it ever come down to someone's life being in danger due to witchcraft, I would wholeheartedly do what was needed and tell Liam the truth. Lives were more important than keeping secrets. Had Kevin Paul done the same in his complicated situation, maybe he would still be alive today.

Tomorrow wasn't guaranteed, so I'd made the decision to take each day as it came and enjoy these moments to the fullest. What mattered most right now was that Lyle Gafney was behind bars and Rye Dolgiram wasn't some evil warlock working for the coven. The residents of Paramour Bay were safe from clowns, humans, and supernatural beings alike for the time being.

You're forgetting something, Raven. Skippy. He's still out there, biding his time...but I'll be ready. Yes, siree, I'll be ready.

~ The End ~

Ghosts, goblins, and ghouls go bump in the night in the latest installment of the Paramour Bay Mysteries by USA Today Bestselling Author Kennedy Layne...

The residents in the small coastal town of Paramour Bay are sorting through their unwanted belongings and setting up card tables in their driveways in order to get ready for their annual community garage sale.

Raven Marigold hasn't lived in town long enough to contribute to the garage sale, but she sure is ready to find some basement bargains. Armed with a small reserve of cash and a large tote for her treasure trove, she wasn't prepared for her familiar to make a shocking discovery of an authentic sapphire pendant. You see, the disturbing part of such a find was that the pendant belonged to a resident...one who'd been buried with it.

A haunted cemetery, an empty crypt, and a rather curious raccoon are all cryptic clues in another magical mystery that will leave you gasping for breath until the very last page!

Other Series By Kennedy Layne

Detective Kinsley Aspen Novels

Hadley Dawkins Novels

Touch of Evil Series

The Graveside Mysteries

The Widow Taker Trilogy

Paramour Bay Mysteries

Hex on Me Mysteries

The Safeguard Series

Keys to Love Series

Office Roulette Trilogy

Surviving Ashes Series

Red Starr Series

CSA Case Files

About the Author

Kennedy Layne, a USA Today bestselling author, resides in the Midwest with her retired Marine Master Sergeant husband and their menagerie of pets. Fueled by coffee and her love for thrillers, cozy mysteries, and romantic suspense novels, Kennedy loves to spend time in front of her fireplace crafting stories that keep her readers guessing until the very end.

Email:
kennedylayneauthor@gmail.com

Website:
www.kennedylayne.com

Newsletter:
www.kennedylayne.com/newsletter.html

www.ingramcontent.com/pod-product-compliance
Lightning Source LLC
Chambersburg PA
CBHW071134200626
46817CB00018B/2945